THE WHITE MOUNTAINS

Also by John Christopher
Available from Aladdin

The Tripods:
The City of Gold and Lead
The Pool of Fire
When the Tripods Came

JOHN CHRISTOPHER

THE TRIPODS

THE WHITE MOUNTAINS

Aladdin

NEW YORK   LONDON   TORONTO   SYDNEY   NEW DELHI

ALADDIN

An imprint of Simon & Schuster Children's Publishing Division
1230 Avenue of the Americas, New York, NY 10020
This Aladdin hardcover edition May 2014
Text copyright © 1967 by John Christopher
Jacket illustration copyright © 2014 by Anton Petrov
All rights reserved, including the right of reproduction in whole or in part in any form.
ALADDIN is a trademark of Simon & Schuster, Inc., and related logo is a registered trademark of Simon & Schuster, Inc.
Also available in an Aladdin paperback edition.
For information about special discounts for bulk purchases, please contact Simon & Schuster Special Sales at 1-866-506-1949 or business@simonandschuster.com.
The Simon & Schuster Speakers Bureau can bring authors to your live event. For more information or to book an event contact the Simon & Schuster Speakers Bureau at 1-866-248-3049 or visit our website at www.simonspeakers.com.
Jacket design by Karin Paprocki
Interior design by Hilary Zarycky
The text of this book was set in Venetian 301.
Manufactured in the United States of America 0414 FFG
2 4 6 8 10 9 7 5 3 1
Library of Congress Control Number 2002070808
ISBN 978-1-4814-1478-4 (hc)
ISBN 978-1-4814-1477-7 (pbk)
ISBN 978-1-4424-2722-8 (eBook)

To Jessica:
this, and the rest, with love

CONTENTS

CONTENTS

PREFACE
WHAT IS A TRIPOD?

Well, there's a brief description in the first chapter of *The White Mountains*: ". . . we could see it over the roofs of the houses to the south: the great hemisphere of gleaming metal rocking through the air above the three articulated legs, several times as high as the church. Its shadow came before it, and fell on us when it halted, two of its legs astride the river and the mill. . . . one of the enormous burnished tentacles came down, gently and precisely, and its tip curled about Jack's waist, and it lifted him up, up, to where a hole opened like a mouth in the hemisphere, and swallowed him."

So a Tripod is a monstrous machine, some sixty feet high. It travels on three metal legs and has tentacles (three, we discover later) which can reach down and sweep a boy up into an opening in the metal pod which seems to represent its head. But is a Tripod an intelligent machine? Or some extraordinary form of transportation? And if the latter, are there creatures inside the pod, driving this weird sort of tank on stilts the way we might drive a car?

At the end of *The White Mountains*, the reader may have his or her own guess about exactly what kind of thing a Tripod is, but he or she doesn't really know. I'll let you into a secret: at that point the writer didn't know, either.

Thirty-five years ago I received a letter which was to prove much more important than it seemed at the time. By then I had been a professional writer for over ten years, writing different kinds of fiction but principally what was commonly known as science fiction.

The letter was from my London agent. A publisher who had read my adult novels was wondering if I would write something for a younger audience. This would be a new departure for me, and I wasn't sure I wanted to get involved. But it was encouraging that someone was actually asking me to write something, instead of just waiting till I sent a manuscript in. I also reckoned that, children's novels being normally much shorter, I wouldn't be squandering more than a month of precious writing time.

But what sort of a book was it going to be? The publisher obviously wanted science fiction, but I was getting tired of destroying the world—by famine or freezing or earthquakes—and I was no longer interested in exploring the universe outside our planet. There was a reason for that.

When I was the age of the boys and girls for whom it was now proposed I write, I'd been very excited about the possibilities of space travel, but those had been different days. In the early thirties we knew just enough about the solar system for its possibilities to be a magnet to the imagination. The Moon might be cold and dead, but the planets offered scope for dreaming. Mars, for instance, was colder than our earth and had a thinner atmosphere, but possibly not too cold or airless to support life.

And Mars had those canals. An Italian astronomer called Schiaparelli, looking through his telescope in the nineteenth century, said he had seen *canali* on Mars's rust-red surface. In Italian that just meant "channels," but it got translated as "canals," which was much more intriguing. Maybe in that thin but breathable atmosphere there were long waterways, built by an ancient race of Martians, dotted with Martian cities that were lit by day by a smaller sun and at night by the magic gleam of two low-lying moons. An ancient race, because one might suppose that on that chillier planet the process of life's evolution had been in advance of ours. Apart from being older, the Martians might well be wiser and able to pass on to us the fruits of their knowledge. Or, if they were so ancient as to have become extinct, the ruins of their cities might still be there to be explored.

Then there was Venus—closer to the sun and much hotter than the earth—with its perpetual blanket of clouds. What might lie beneath the clouds? Perhaps a planet in an earlier period of evolution, as Mars was in a later one. Something like our own Carboniferous era, perhaps. Did tropical swamps teeming with dinosaurs and hovering pterodactyls await the arrival of our first spaceship?

Because that was something else we felt confident about: early experiments with rockets had already made the eventual conquest of space more than plausible. It could happen in our lifetime, and with it bring unthinkable wonders. It was a bit like being in Elizabethan England, reading stories about what might be found in the new world which was opening up on the far side of the barely explored western ocean.

But in three short decades everything changed. By the 1960s we knew more about the universe and the solar system—but what we'd learned was much less interesting than what we'd imagined. We knew that Mars was not just cold but an altogether hostile environment, Venus a choking oven of poisonous gases. The chance of any kind of life existing on either planet—or anywhere within reach of our probing rockets—was incredibly remote. That brave new world on the other side of the ocean of space had turned into a lifeless desert.

A couple of years after I wrote *The White Mountains,* space itself was finally conquered. The landing on the Moon was televised around the world, timed to coincide with prime-time U.S. television viewing. That meant the early hours of the morning in the Channel Islands, where I then lived. The boy I had been at fourteen would never have believed that I couldn't be bothered to stay up to watch it.

I had seen the future, and found it disappointing; so what remained? Well, there was the past. The color which had bleached out of our interplanetary speculations was still bright in human history and there was life there, and romance and action. I doubted if my inquiring publisher would be much impressed by getting a story set in feudal England, but there might be a way around that.

Imagine a race of aliens who conquer the earth. They have a means of controlling their human slaves, which involves putting a metal Cap on their heads when they reach puberty. Through the Cap they can subdue people individually, suppressing rebellious impulses. To exercise a more general control they need to impose a social organization which is orderly and hierarchical. The chaotic capitalist system which they first encounter, with its emphasis on individual enterprise, is not suitable for this purpose. So they delve into human history and find a system which is. Out go bankers and inventors and those awkward types who just want to do something different; back come kings and nobles, farmers and peasants—people accustomed to order imposed from above, in a world which only changes with the seasons.

The publisher wanted the future; I was more interested in the past. I reckoned I might satisfy both of us by combining the two, in a medieval world threatened and dominated by monstrous futuristic machines.

Somehow it worked. Over and over again in the letters I've had from young readers there have been comments along these lines: "What really got me about the book was not knowing whether I was in the past or the future."

So I wrote *The White Mountains* and sent it off. The London publisher approved of it. Another copy went to New York. My agent there wrote back to say he had offered the book to a children's book publisher, who had turned it down but said they might be interested if I rewrote it. He enclosed a long letter from the children's books editor.

Basically, what she said was that she loved the first chapter but the rest of the book was a mess: it would need a complete reworking from Chapter 2 onward. This was something that had not happened to me before. My adult novels had either been taken or rejected as they stood. I was not used to rewriting and certainly not eager to start doing so with a mere children's book. Macmillan had been the first U.S. publisher to see the book; another firm might take a different view.

Then I read thoroughly the letter I'd previously only skimmed. I realized the observations were sharp, the suggestions very much to the point. And I was forced to accept that my own attitude had been badly flawed. I was to learn a hard but invaluable lesson: there's no such thing as a "mere children's book," and children's book editors are some of the brightest and most dedicated people in the field. So, after fuming a little, I went back to work and rewrote the book from the end of Chapter 1. I sent the revised version to the London publisher, who said yes again. Then it came back from New York with another letter: The beginning and the end were okay, but the middle was still wrong. I sighed, and went back to the typewriter. The third version met her high critical standards. The London publisher simply agreed yet again.

It isn't easy to start an apprenticeship when you are the author of thirty published books, but it's certainly good for you. With the sequel, *The City of Gold and Lead*, the New York editor only asked me to rewrite the beginning. When she received *The Pool of Fire*, the last book in the trilogy, she cabled an immediate acceptance.

I thought then that I'd licked it, but I still had a lot to learn about writing for young people. The next book I wrote was rejected as a total mess, only salvaged when my American and British editors brought me to London and sat over me till we (one of them, actually) came up with a solution to the chief and seemingly intractable problem. Over the years I was to be grateful for much advice and help from children's book editors, something I had never encountered while writing my thirty previous adult books.

My editor in New York was Susan Hirschman. The original version of *The White Mountains* was probably just about worth publishing: the London editor thought so. But would it, without Susan, have remained in print and worthy of a commemorative relaunch, three and a half decades after its original publication? I've no doubt about the answer to that.

—*John Christopher, 2003*

THE WHITE MOUNTAINS

ONE

CAPPING DAY

APART FROM THE ONE IN THE CHURCH TOWER, there were five clocks in the village that kept reasonable time, and my father owned one of them. It stood on the mantelpiece in the parlor, and every night before he went to bed he took the key from a vase, and wound it up. Once a year the clockman came from Winchester, on an old jogging packhorse, to clean and oil it and put it right. Afterward he would drink camomile tea with my mother, and tell her the news of the city and what he had learned in the villages through which he had passed. My father, if he were not busy milling, would stalk out at this time, with some contemptuous remark about gossip; but later, in the evening, I would hear my mother passing the stories on to him. He did not show much enthusiasm, but he listened to them.

My father's great treasure, though, was not the clock, but the Watch. This, a miniature clock with a dial less than an inch across and a circlet permitting it to be worn on the wrist, was kept in a locked drawer of his desk; and only brought out to be worn on ceremonial occasions, like Harvest Festival, or a Capping. The clockman was only allowed to see to it every third year, and at such times my father stood by, watching him as he worked. There was no other Watch in the village, nor in any of the villages round about. The clockman said there were a number in Winchester, but none as fine as this. I wondered if he said it to please my father, who certainly showed pleasure in the hearing, but I believe it truly was of very good workmanship. The body of the Watch was of a steel much superior to anything they could make at the forge in Alton, and the works inside were a wonder of intricacy and skill. On the front was printed "Anti-magnetique Incabloc," which we supposed must have been the name of the craftsman who made it in olden times.

The clockman had visited us the week before, and I had been permitted to look on for a time while he cleaned and oiled the Watch. The sight fascinated me, and after he had gone I found my thoughts running continually on this treasure, now locked away again in its drawer. I was, of course, forbidden to touch my father's desk and the notion of opening a locked drawer in it should have been unthinkable. Nonetheless, the idea persisted. And after a day or two, I admitted to myself that it was only the fear of being caught that prevented me.

On Saturday morning, I found myself alone in the house. My father was in the mill room, grinding, and the servants—even Molly who normally did not leave the house during the day—had been brought in to help. My mother was out visiting old Mrs. Ash, who was sick, and would be gone an hour at least. I had finished my homework, and there was nothing to stop my going out into the bright May morning and finding Jack. But what completely filled my mind was the thought that I had this opportunity to look at the Watch, with small chance of detection.

The key, I had observed, was kept with the other keys in a small box beside my father's bed. There were four, and the third one opened the drawer. I took out the Watch, and gazed at it. It was not going, but I knew one wound it and set the hands by means of the small knob at one side. If I were to wind it only a couple of turns it would run down quite soon—just in case my father decided to look at it later in the day. I did this, and listened to its quiet rhythmic ticking. Then I set the hands by the clock. After that it only remained for me to slip it on my wrist. Even notched to the first hole, the leather strap was loose; but I was wearing the Watch.

Having achieved what I had thought was an ulti-mate ambition, I found, as I think is often the case, that there remained something more. To wear it was a tri-umph, but to be seen wearing it . . . I had told my cousin, Jack Leeper, that I would meet him that morn-ing, in the old ruins at the end of the village. Jack, who was nearly a year older than myself and due to be pre-sented at the next Capping, was the person, next to my parents, that I most admired. To take the Watch out of the house was to add enormity to disobedience, but having already gone so far, it was easier to contemplate it. My mind made up, I was determined to waste none of the precious time I had. I opened the front door, stuck the hand with the Watch deep into my trouser pocket, and ran off down the street.

The village lay at a crossroads, with the road in which our house stood running alongside the river (this giving power for the mill, of course) and the second road crossing it at the ford. Beside the ford stood a small wooden bridge for foot travelers, and I pelted across, noticing that the river was higher than usual from the spring rains. My Aunt Lucy was approaching the bridge as I left it at the far end. She called a greeting to me, and I called back, having first taken care to veer to the other side of the road. The baker's shop was there, with trays of buns and cakes set out, and it was reasonable that I should be heading that way: I had a couple of pennies in my pocket. But I ran on past it, and did not slacken to a walk until I had reached the point where the houses thinned out and at last ended.

The ruins were a hundred yards farther on. On

one side of the road lay Spiller's meadow, with cows grazing, but on my side there was a thorn hedge, and a potato field beyond. I passed a gap in the hedge, not looking in my concentration on what I was going to show Jack, and was startled a moment later by a shout from behind me. I recognized the voice as Henry Parker's.

Henry, like Jack, was a cousin of mine—my name is Will Parker—but, unlike Jack, no friend. (I had several cousins in the village: people did not usually travel far to marry.) He was a month younger than I, but taller and heavier, and we had hated each other as long as I could remember. When it came to fighting, as it very often did, I was outmatched physically, and had to rely on agility and quickness if I were not going to be beaten. From Jack I had learned some skill in wrestling which, in the past year, had enabled me to hold my own more, and in our last encounter I had thrown him heavily enough to wind him and leave him gasping for breath. But for wrestling one needed the use of both hands. I thrust my left hand deeper into the pocket and, not answering his call, ran on toward the ruins.

He was closer than I had thought, though, and he pounded after me, yelling threats. I put a spurt on, looked back to see how much of a lead I had, and found myself slipping on a patch of mud. (Cobbles were laid inside the village, but out here the road was in its usual poor condition, aggravated by the rains.) I fought desperately to keep my footing, but would not, until it was too late, bring out my other hand to help balance myself. As a result, I went slithering and sprawling and finally fell. Before I could recover, Henry was kneeling across me, holding the back of my head with his hand and pushing my face down into the mud.

This activity would normally have kept him happy for some time, but he found something of greater interest. I had instinctively used both hands to protect myself as I fell, and he saw the Watch on my wrist. In a moment he had wrenched it off, and stood up to examine it. I scrambled to my feet, and made a grab, but he held it easily above his head and out of my reach.

I said, panting, "Give that back!"

"It's not yours," he said. "It's your father's."

I was in agony in case the Watch had been damaged, broken maybe, in my fall, but even so I attempted to get my leg between his, to drop him. He parried, and, stepping back, said,

"Keep your distance." He braced himself, as though preparing to throw a stone. "Or I'll see how far I can fling it."

"If you do," I said, "you'll get a whipping for it."

There was a grin on his fleshy face. "So will you. And your father lays on heavier than mine does. I'll tell you what: I'll borrow it for a while. Maybe I'll let you have it back this afternoon. Or tomorrow."

"Someone will see you with it."

He grinned again. "I'll risk that."

I made a grab at him. I had decided that he was bluffing about throwing it away. I almost got him off balance, but not quite. We swayed and struggled, and then crashed together and rolled down into the ditch by the side of the road. There was some water in it, but we went on fighting, even after a voice challenged us from above. Jack—for it was he who had called to us to get up—had to come down and pull us apart by force. This was not difficult for him. He was as big as Henry, and tremendously strong also. He dragged us back up to the road, got to the root of the matter, took the Watch off Henry, and dismissed him with a clip across the back of the neck.

I said tearfully, "Is it all right?"

"I think so." He examined it, and handed it to me. "But you were a fool to bring it out."

"I wanted to show it to you."

"Not worth it," he said briefly. "Anyway, we'd better see about getting it back. I'll lend a hand."

Jack had always been around to lend a hand, as long as I could remember. It was strange, I thought, as we walked toward the village, that in just over a week's time I would be on my own. The Capping would have taken place, and Jack would be a boy no longer.

Jack stood guard while I put the Watch back and returned the drawer key to the place where I had found it. I changed my wet and dirty trousers and shirt, and we retraced our steps to the ruins. No one knew what these buildings had once been, and I think one of the things that attracted us was a sign, printed on a chipped and rusted metal plate:

DANGER

6,600 VOLTS

We had no idea what Volts had been, but the notion of danger, however far away and long ago, was exciting. There was more lettering, but for the most part the rust had destroyed it. LECT CITY: we wondered if that were the city it had come from.

Farther along was the den Jack had made. One approached it through a crumbling arch; inside it was dry, and there was a place to build a fire. Jack had made one before coming out to look for me, and had skinned, cleaned, and skewered a rabbit ready for us to grill. There would be food in plenty at home— the midday meal on a Saturday was always lavish— but this did not prevent my looking forward greedily to roast rabbit with potatoes baked in the embers of the fire. Nor would it stop me doing justice to the steak pie my mother had in the oven. Although on the small side, I had a good appetite.

We watched and smelled the rabbit cooking in companionable silence. We could get on very well together without much conversation, though normally I had a ready tongue. Too ready, perhaps—I knew that a lot of the trouble with Henry arose because I could not avoid trying to get a rise out of him whenever possible.

Jack was not much of a talker under any circumstances, but to my surprise, after a time he broke the silence. His talk was inconsequential at first, chatter about events that had taken place in the village, but I had the feeling that he was trying to get around to something else, something more important. Then he stopped, stared in silence for a second or two at the crisping carcass, and said,

"This place will be yours, after the Capping."

It was difficult to know what to say. I suppose if I had thought about it at all, I would have expected that he would pass the den on to me, but I had not thought about it. One did not think much about things connected with the Cappings, and certainly did not talk about them. For Jack, of all people, to do so was surprising, but what he said next was more surprising still.

"In a way," he said, "I almost hope it doesn't work. I'm not sure I wouldn't rather be a Vagrant."

I should say something about the Vagrants. Every village generally had a few—at that time there were four in ours, as far as I knew—but the number was constantly changing as some moved off and others took their place. They occasionally did a little work, but whether they did or not the village supported them. They lived in the Vagrant House, which in our case stood on the corner where the two roads crossed and was larger than all but a handful of houses (my father's being one). It could easily have accommodated a dozen Vagrants, and there had been times when there had been almost that many there. Food was supplied to them—it was not luxurious, but adequate—and a servant looked after the place. Other servants were sent to lend a hand when the House filled up.

What was known, though not discussed, was that the Vagrants were people for whom the Capping had proved a failure. They had Caps, as normal people did, but they were not working properly. If this were going to happen, it usually showed itself in the first day or two following a Capping: the person who had been Capped showed distress, which increased as the days went by, turning at last into a fever of the brain. In this state, they were clearly in much pain. Fortunately the crisis did not last long; fortunately also, it happened only rarely. The great majority of Cappings were entirely successful. I suppose only about one in twenty produced a Vagrant.

When he was well again, the Vagrant would start his wanderings. He, or she; because it happened occasionally with girls, although much more rarely. Whether it was because they saw themselves as being outside the community of normal people, or because the fever had left a permanent restlessness in them, I did not know. But off they would go and wander through the land, stopping a day here, as long as a month there, but always moving on. Their minds, certainly, had been affected. None of them could settle to a train of thought for long, and many had visions, and did strange things.

They were taken for granted, and looked after, but, like the Cappings, not much talked about. Children, generally, viewed them with suspicion and avoided them. They, for their part, mostly seemed melancholy, and did not talk much, even to each other. It was a great shock to hear Jack say he half wished to be a Vagrant, and I did not know how to answer him. But he did not seem to need a response. He said, "The Watch—do you ever think what it must have been like in the days when things like that were made?"

I had, from time to time, but it was another subject on which speculation was not encouraged, and Jack had never talked in this way before. I said, "Before the Tripods?"

"Yes."

"Well, we know it was the Black Age. There were too many people, and not enough food, so that people starved, and fought each other, and there were all kinds of sicknesses, and . . ."

"And things like the Watch were made—by men, not the Tripods."

"We don't know that."

"Do you remember," he asked, "four years ago, when I went to stay with my Aunt Matilda?"

I remembered. She was his aunt, not mine, even

though we were cousins: she had married a foreigner. Jack said, "She lives at Bishopstoke, on the other side of Winchester. I went out one day, walking, and I came to the sea. There were the ruins of a city that must have been twenty times as big as Winchester."

I knew of the ruined great-cities of the ancients, of course. But these, too, were little talked of, and then with disapproval and a shade of dread. No one would dream of going near them. It was disquieting even to think of looking at one, as Jack had done. I said, "Those were the cities where all the murdering and sickness were."

"So we are told. But I saw something there. It was the hulk of a ship, rusting away so that in places you could see right through it. And it was bigger than the village. Much bigger."

I fell silent. I was trying to imagine it, to see it in my mind as he had seen it in reality. But my mind could not accept it.

Jack said, "And that was built by men. Before the Tripods came."

Again I was at a loss for words. In the end, I said lamely, "People are happy now."

Jack turned the rabbit on the spit. After a while, he said, "Yes. I suppose you're right."

The weather stayed fine until Capping Day. From morning till night people worked in the fields, cutting the grass for hay. There had been so much rain earlier that it stood high and luxuriant, a promise of good winter fodder. The Day itself, of course, was a holiday. After breakfast, we went to church, and the parson preached on the rights and duties of manhood, into which Jack was to enter. Not of womanhood, because there was no girl to be Capped. Jack, in fact, stood alone, dressed in the white tunic which was prescribed. I looked at him, wondering how he was feeling, but whatever his emotions were, he did not show them.

Not even when, the service over, we stood out in the street in front of the church, waiting for the Tripod. The bells were ringing the Capping Peal, but apart from that all was quiet. No one talked or whispered or smiled. It was, we knew, a great experience for everyone who had been Capped. Even the Vagrants came and stood in the same rapt silence.

But for us children, the time lagged desperately. And for Jack, apart from everyone, in the middle of the street? I felt for the first time a shiver of fear, in the realization that at the next Capping I would be standing there. I would not be alone, of course, because Henry was to be presented with me. There was not much consolation in that thought.

At last we heard, above the clang of bells, the deep staccato booming in the distance, and there was a kind of sigh from everyone. The booming came nearer and then, suddenly, we could see it over the roofs of the houses to the south: the great hemi-sphere of gleaming metal rocking through the air above the three articulated legs, several times as high as the church. Its shadow came before it, and fell on us when it halted, two of its legs astride the river and the mill. We waited, and I was shivering in earnest now, unable to halt the tremors that ran through my body.

Sir Geoffrey, the Lord of our Manor, stepped forward and made a small stiff bow in the direction of the Tripod; he was an old man, and could not bend much nor easily. And so one of the enormous burnished tentacles came down, gently and precisely, and its tip curled about Jack's waist, and it lifted him up, up, to where a hole opened like a mouth in the hemisphere, and swallowed him.

In the afternoon there were games, and people moved about the village, visiting, laughing, and talking, and the young men and women who were unmarried strolled together in the fields. Then, in the evening, there was the Feast, with tables set up in the street since the weather held fair, and the smell of roast beef mixing with the smells of beer and cider and lemonade, and all kinds of cakes and puddings. Lamps were hung outside the houses; in the dusk they would be lit, and glow like yellow blossoms along the street. But before the Feast started, Jack was brought back to us.

There was the distant booming first, and the quietness and waiting, and the tread of the gigantic feet, shaking the earth. The Tripod halted as before, and the mouth opened in the side of the hemisphere, and then the tentacle swept down and carefully set Jack by the place which had been left for him at

Sir Geoffrey's right hand. I was a long way away, with the children at the far end, but I could see him clearly. He looked pale, but otherwise his face did not seem any different. The difference was in his white shaved head, on which the darker metal tracery of the Cap stood out like a spider's web. His hair would soon grow again, over and around the metal, and, with thick black hair such as he had, in a few months the Cap would be almost unnoticeable. But it would be there all the same, a part of him now till the day he died.

This, though, was the moment of rejoicing and making merry. He was a man, and tomorrow would do a man's work and get a man's pay. They cut the choicest fillet of beef and brought it to him, with a frothing tankard of ale, and Sir Geoffrey toasted his health and fortune. I forgot my earlier fears, and envied him, and thought how next year I would be there, a man myself.

I did not see Jack the next day, but the day after that we met when, having finished my homework, I was on my way to the den. He was with four or five other men, coming back from the fields. I called him, and he smiled and, after a moment's hesitation, let the others go on. We stood facing each other, only a few yards from the place where, little more than a week earlier, he had separated Henry and me. But things were very different.

I said, "How are you?"

It was not just a polite question. By now, if the Capping were going to fail, he would be feeling the pains and discomfort that would lead, in due course, to his becoming a Vagrant. He said, "I'm fine, Will."

I hesitated, and blurted out, "What was it like?"

He shook his head. "You know it's not permitted to talk about that. But I can promise you that you won't be hurt."

I said, "But why?"

"Why what?"

"Why should the Tripods take people away, and Cap them? What right have they?"

"They do it for our good."

"But I don't see why it has to happen. I'd sooner stay as I am."

He smiled. "You can't understand now, but you

will understand when it happens. It's . . ." He shook his head. "I can't describe it."

"Jack," I said, "I've been thinking." He waited, without much interest. "Of what you said—about the wonderful things that men made, before the Tripods."

"That was nonsense," he said, and turned and walked on to the village. I watched him for a time and then, feeling very much alone, made my way to the den.

TWO

MY NAME IS OZYMANDIAS

I**T WAS NOT UNTIL AFTER HIS CAPPING THAT I** understood how much I had depended on Jack for companionship in the past. Our alliance had isolated me from other boys of roughly my age in and around the village. I suppose it would have been possible to overcome this—Joe Beith, the carpenter's son, made overtures of friendship, for one—but in the mood I was in I preferred to be alone. I used to go down to the den and sit there for hours, thinking about it all. Henry came once, and made some jeering remarks, and we fought. My anger was so great that I beat him decisively, and he kept out of my way after that.

From time to time I met Jack, and we exchanged words that meant nothing. His manner to me was amiable and distant: it carried the hint of a friendship suspended, a suggestion that he was waiting on the far side of a gulf which in due course I would cross, and that then everything would be as it had been before. This did not comfort me, though, for the person I missed was the old Jack, and he was gone forever. As I would be? The thought frightened me, and I tried to dismiss it, but it continually returned.

Somehow, in this doubt and fear and brooding, I found myself becoming interested in the Vagrants. I remembered Jack's remark and wondered what he would have been like if the Capping had not worked. By now he would probably have left the village. I looked at the Vagrants who were staying with us, and thought of them as once being like Jack and myself, in their own villages, sane and happy and with plans for the future. I was my father's only son, and would be expected to take over the mill from him one day. But if the Capping were not a success . . .

There were three of them, two recently arrived and a third who had been with us several weeks. He was a man of my father's age, but his beard was unkempt, his hair gray and sparse, with the lines of the Cap showing through it. He spent his time collecting stones from the fields near the village, and with them he was building a cairn outside the Vagrant House. He collected perhaps twenty stones a day, each about the size of a half brick. It was impossible to understand why he chose one stone rather than another, or what the purpose of the cairn was. He spoke very little, using words as a child learning to talk does.

The other two were much younger, one of them probably no more than a year from his Capping. He talked a lot, and what he said seemed almost to make sense, but never quite did. The third, a few years older, could talk in a way that one understood, but did not often do so. He seemed sunk in a great sadness, and would lie in the road beside the House all day, staring up at the sky.

He remained when the others moved on, the young one in the morning and the cairn-builder in the afternoon of the same day. The pile of stones stayed there, unfinished and without meaning. I looked at them that evening, and wondered what I would be doing twenty-five years from now. Grinding corn at the mill? Perhaps. Or perhaps wandering the countryside, living on charity and doing useless things. Somehow, the alternatives were not so black and white as I would have expected. I did not know why, but I thought I had a glimmer of understanding what Jack had meant, that morning in the den.

The new Vagrant arrived the next day and, being on my way to the den, I saw him come, along the road from the west. He was in his thirties, I judged, a powerfully built man, with red hair and a beard. He carried an ash stick and the usual small pack on his back, and he was singing a song, quite tunefully, as he strode along. He saw me, and stopped singing.

"Boy," he said, "what is the name of this place?"

"It's called Wherton," I told him.

"Wherton," he repeated. "Ah, loveliest village of the plain; here is no anguish, here no pain. Do you know me, boy?"

I shook my head. "No."

"I am the king of this land. My wife was the queen of a rainy country, but I left her weeping. My name is Ozymandias. Look on my works, ye mighty, and despair."

He talked nonsense, but at least he talked, and the words themselves could be understood. They sounded a bit like poetry, and I remembered the name Ozymandias from a poem which I had found in a book, one of the dozen or so on the shelf in the parlor. As he went on toward the village, I followed him. Glancing back, he said, "Dost follow me, boy? Wouldst be my page? Alas, alas. The fox has his hole, and the bird shelters in the great leafy oak, but the son of man has not where to lay his head. Have you no business of your own, then?"

"Nothing important."

"Nothing is important, true, but how does a man find Nothing? Where shall he seek for it? I tell you, could I find Nothing, I would be not king but emperor. Who dwells in the House, this day and hour?"

I assumed he was talking about the Vagrant House.

"Only one," I said. "I don't know his name."

"His name shall be Star. And yours?"

"Will Parker."

"Will is a good name. What trade does your father follow, Will, for you wear too fine a cloth to be a laborer's son?"

"He keeps the mill."

"And this the burden of his song for ever seems to be: I care for nobody, no, not I, and nobody cares for me. Have you many friends, Will?"

"No. Not many."

"A good answer. For he that proclaims many friends declares that he has none."

I said, on an impulse which surprised me when I reflected on it, "In fact, I don't have any. I had one, but he was Capped a month ago."

He stopped in the road, and I did so, too. We were on the outskirts of the village, opposite the Widow Ingold's cottage. The Vagrant looked at me keenly.

"No business, of importance anyway, and no friend. One who talks and walks with Vagrants. How old are you, Will?"

"Thirteen."

"You are small for it. So you will take the Cap next summer?"

"Yes."

Widow Ingold, I saw, was watching us through the curtains. The Vagrant also flicked a glance in that direction, and suddenly started dancing a weird little jig in the road. He sang, in a cracked voice:

Under the greenwood tree,
Who loves to lie with me,
And tune his merry note
Unto the sweet bird's throat?

All the rest of the way to the Vagrant House he talked nonsense, and I was glad to part from him there.

My preoccupation with the Vagrants had been noticed, and that evening my father took me to task for it. He was sometimes stern but more often kindly—just according to his lights, but he saw the world in simple shades of black and white, and found it hard to be patient with things that struck him as foolishness. There was no sense that he could see in a boy hanging about the Vagrant House: one was sorry for them, and it was a human duty to give them food and shelter, but there it should end. I had been seen that day with the most recent arrival, who appeared to be even madder than most. It was silly, and it gave tongues cause to wag. He hoped he would hear no more such reports, and I was not to go into the Vagrant House on any pretext. Did I understand?

I indicated that I did. There was more to it, I realized, than concern over people talking about me. He might be willing to listen, at a remove, to news from other villages and from the city, but for gossip and ill-natured talk he truly had nothing but contempt.

I wondered if his fear was of something quite different, and much worse. As a boy, he had had an elder brother who had turned Vagrant. This had never been spoken of in our house, but Jack had told me of it long ago. There were some who said that this kind of weakness ran in families; and he might think that my interest in Vagrants was a bad omen for the Capping next year. This was not logical, but I knew that a man impatient of foolishness in others may yet have fallibilities of his own.

What with this, and my own embarrassment at the way in which the new Vagrant had behaved in the presence of others, I made a kind of resolve to do as I had been bid, and for a couple of days kept well clear of the Vagrants. Twice I saw the man who had called himself Ozymandias clowning and talking to himself in the street, and shied off. But on the third day I went to school not by the back way, the path along the riverbank, but out of our front door, past the church. And past the Vagrant House. There was no sign of anyone, but when I came back in the middle of the day, I saw Ozymandias coming from the opposite direction. I quickened my step, and we met at the crossroads.

He said, "Welcome, Will! I have not seen thee, these many days. Has aught ailed thee, boy? A murrain? Or haply the common cold?"

There had been something about him that had interested, even fascinated me, and it was that which had brought me here in the hope of encountering him again. I admitted that but, in the moment of admission, was once more conscious of the things that had kept me away. There was no one in our immediate vicinity, but other children, coming from school, were not far behind me, and there were people who knew me on the far side of the crossroads.

I said, "I've been busy with things," and prepared to move on.

He put a hand on my arm. "Wilt tarry, Will? He that has no friend can travel at his own pace, and pause, when he chooses, for a few minutes' converse."

"I've got to get back," I said. "My dinner will be waiting."

I had looked away from him. After only a slight pause, he dropped his hand.

"Then do not let me keep you, Will, for though man does not live on bread alone, it is bread he must have first."

His tone was cheerful, but I thought I detected something else. Disappointment? I started to walk on, but after a few steps checked and looked back. His eyes were still on me. I said, in a low voice stumbling over the words:

"Do you go out into the fields at all?"

"When the sun shines."

"Farther along the road on which I met you—there's an old ruin, on the right—I have a den there, on the far side where the copse comes close—it has a broken arch for an entrance, and an old red stone outside, like a seat."

He said softly, "I hear, Will. Do you spend much time there?"

"I go there after school, usually."

He nodded. "Do so."

Abruptly, his gaze went from me to the sky, and he held his arms out above his head, and shouted, "And in that year came Jim, the Prophet of Serendipity, and with him a host of angels, riding their white geldings across the sky, raising a dust of clouds and striking sparks from their hooves that burned the wheat in the fields, and the evil in men's hearts. So spake Ozymandias. Selah! Selah! Selah!"

The others were coming up the road from the

school. I left him and hurried toward home. I could hear him shouting until I passed the church.

I went to the den after school with mingled feelings of anticipation and unease. My father had said he hoped he would hear no more reports of my mixing with Vagrants, and had placed a direct prohibition on my going to the Vagrant House. I had obeyed the second part, and was taking steps to avoid the first, but I was under no illusion that he would regard this as anything but willful disobedience. And to what end? The opportunity of talking to a man whose conversation was a hodge-podge of sense and nonsense, with the latter very much predominating. It was not worth it.

And yet, remembering the keen blue eyes under the mass of red hair, I could not help feeling that there was something about this man that made the risk, and the disobedience, worthwhile. I kept a sharp lookout on my way to the ruins, and called out as I approached the den. But there was no one there; nor for a good time after that. I began to think he was not coming—that his wits were so addled that he had failed to take my meaning, or forgotten it altogether—when I heard a twig snap and, peering out, saw Ozymandias. He was less than ten yards from the entrance. He was not singing, or talking, but moving quietly, almost stealthily.

A new fear struck me then. There were tales that a Vagrant once, years ago, had murdered children in a dozen villages, before he was caught and hanged. Could they be true, and could this be such another? I had invited him here, telling no one, and a cry for help would not be heard as far from the village as this. I froze against the wall of the den, tensing myself for a rush that might carry me past him to the comparative safety of the open.

But a single glance at him as he looked in reassured me. Whether mad or not, I was sure this was a man to be trusted. The lines in his face were the lines of good humor. He said, "So I have found you, Will." He glanced about him, in approval. "You have a snug place here."

"My cousin Jack did most of it. He is better with his hands than I am."

"The one that was Capped this summer?"

"Yes."

"You watched the Capping?" I nodded. "How is he, since then?"

"Well," I said, "but different."

"Having become a man."

"Not only that."

"Tell me."

I hesitated a moment, but in voice and gesture as well as face he inspired confidence. He was also, I realized, talking naturally and sensibly, with none of the strange words and archaic phrases he had used previously. I began to talk, disjointedly at first and then with more ease, of what Jack had said, and of my own later perplexity. He listened, nodding at times but not interrupting. When I had finished, he said, "Tell me, Will—what do you think of the Tripods?"

I said truthfully, "I don't know. I used to take them for granted—and I was frightened of them, I suppose—but now . . . There are questions in my mind."

"Have you put them to your elders?"

"What good would it do? No one talks about the Tripods. One learns that as a child."

"Shall I answer them for you?" he asked. "Such as I can answer."

There was one thing I was sure of, and I blurted it out: "You are not a Vagrant!"

He smiled. "It depends what meaning you give that word. I go from place to place, as you see. And I behave strangely."

"But to deceive people, not because you cannot help it. Your mind has not been changed."

"No. Not as the minds of the Vagrants are. Nor as your cousin Jack's was, either."

"But you have been Capped!"

He touched the mesh of metal, under his thatch of red hair.

"Agreed. But not by the Tripods. By men—free men."

Bewildered, I said, "I don't understand."

"How could you? But listen, and I will tell you. The Tripods, first. Do you know what they are?" I shook my head, and he went on, "Nor do we, as a certainty. There are two stories about them. One is that they were machines, made by men, which revolted against men and enslaved them."

"In the old days? The days of the giant ship, of the great-cities?"

"Yes. It is a story I find hard to believe, because I do not see how men could give intelligence to machines. The other story is that they do not come originally from this world, but another."

"Another world?"

I was lost again. He said, "They teach you nothing about the stars in school, do they? That is something that perhaps makes the second story more likely to be the true one. You are not told that the stars at night—all the hundreds of thousands of them—are suns like our own sun, and that some may have planets circling them, as our earth circles this sun."

I was confused, my head spinning with the idea. I said, "Is this true?"

"Quite true. And it may be that the Tripods came, in the first place, from one of those worlds. It may be that the Tripods themselves are only vehicles, for creatures who travel inside them. We have never seen the inside of a Tripod, so we do not know."

"And the Caps?"

"Are the means by which they keep men docile and obedient to them."

At first thought, it was incredible. Later, it seemed incredible that I had not seen this before. But all my life Capping had been something I had taken for granted. All my elders were Capped, and contented to be so. It was the mark of the adult, the ceremony itself solemn and linked in one's mind with the holiday and the feast. Despite the few who suffered pain and became Vagrants, it was a duty to which every child looked forward. Only lately, as one could begin to count the months remaining, had there been any doubts in my mind; and the doubts had been ill-formed and difficult to sustain against the weight of adult assurance. Jack had had doubts, too, and then, with the Capping, they had gone. I said, "They make men think the things the Tripods want them to think?"

"They control the brain. How, or to what extent, we are not sure. As you know, the metal is joined to the flesh, so that it cannot be removed. It seems that certain general orders are given when the Cap is put on. Later, specific orders can be given to specific people, but as far as the majority are concerned, they do not seem to bother."

"How do the Vagrants happen?"

"That again is something at which we can only guess. It may be that some minds are weak to start with, and crumble under the strain. Or perhaps the reverse: too strong, so that they fight against domination until they break."

I thought of that, and shuddered. A voice inside one's head, inescapable and irresistible. Anger burned in me, not only for the Vagrants but for all the others—my parents and elders, Jack . . .

"You spoke of free men," I said. "Then the Tripods do not rule all the earth?"

"Near enough all. There are no lands without them, if that's what you mean. Listen, when the Tripods first came—or when they revolted—there were terrible happenings. Cities were destroyed like anthills, and millions on millions were killed or starved to death."

Millions . . . I tried to envision it, but could not. Our village, which was reckoned no small place, numbered about four hundred souls. There were some thirty thousand living in and around the city of Winchester. I shook my head.

He went on, "Those that were left the Tripods Capped, and once Capped they served the Tripods and helped to kill or capture other men. So, within a generation, things were much as they are now. But in one place, at least, a few men escaped. Far to the south, across the sea, there are high mountains, so high that snow lies on them all the year round. The Tripods keep to low ground—perhaps because they travel over it more easily, or because they do not like the thin air higher up—and these are places which men who are alert and free can defend against the Capped who live in the surrounding valleys. In fact, we raid their farms for our food."

"We? So you come from there?" He nodded. "And the Cap you wear?"

"Taken from a dead man. I shaved my head, and it was molded to fit my skull. Once my hair had grown again, it was hard to tell it from a true Cap. But it gives no commands."

"So you can travel as a Vagrant," I said, "and no one suspects you. But why? With what purpose?"

"Partly to see things, and report what I see. But there is something more important. I came for you."

I was startled. "For me?"

"You, and others like you. Those who are not yet Capped, but who are old enough to ask questions and understand answers. And to make a long, difficult, perhaps dangerous journey."

"To the south?"

"To the south. To the White Mountains. With a hard life at the journey's end. But a free one. Well?"

"You will take me there?"

"No. I am not ready to go back yet. And it would be more dangerous. A boy traveling on his own could be an ordinary runaway, but one traveling with a Vagrant . . . you must go on your own. If you decide to go."

"The sea," I said, "how do I cross that?"

He stared at me, and smiled. "The easiest part. And I can give you some help for the rest, too." He brought something from his pocket and showed it to me. "Do you know what this is?"

I nodded. "I have seen one. A compass. The needle points always to the north."

"And this."

He put his hand inside his tunic. There was a hole in the stitching, and he put his fingers down, grasped something, and drew it out. It was a long cylinder of parchment, which he unrolled and spread out on the floor, putting a stone on one end and holding the other. I saw a drawing on it, but it made no sense.

"This is called a map," he said. "The Capped do not need them, so you have not seen one before. It tells you how to reach the White Mountains. Look, there. That signifies the sea. And here, at the bottom, the mountains."

He explained all the things on the map, describing the landmarks I should look for and telling me how to use the compass to find my way. And for the last part of the journey, beyond the Great Lake, he gave me instructions, which I had to memorize. This in case the map were discovered. He said, "But guard it well, in any case. Can you make a hole in the lining of your tunic, as I have done?"

"Yes. I'll keep it safe."

"That leaves only the sea crossing. Go to this

town." He pointed to it. "You will find fishing boats in the harbor. The *Orion* is owned by one of us. A tall man, very swarthy, with a long nose and thin lips. His name is Curtis, Captain Curtis. Go to him. He will get you across the sea. That is where the hard part begins. They speak a different language there. You must keep from being seen, or spoken to, and learn to steal your food as you go."

"I can do that. Do you speak their language?"

"It, and others. Such as your own. It was for that reason I was given this mission." He smiled. "I can be a madman in four tongues."

I said, "I came to you. If I had not . . ."

"I would have found you. I have some skill in discovering the right kind of boy. But you can help me now. Is there any other in these parts that you think might be worth the tackling?"

I shook my head. "No, no one."

He stood up, stretching his legs and rubbing his knee.

"Then tomorrow I will move on. Give me a week before you leave, so that no one suspects a link between us."

"Before you go . . ."

"Yes?"

"Why did they not destroy men altogether, instead of Capping them?"

He shrugged. "We can't read their minds. There are many possible reasons. Part of the food you grow here goes to men who work underground, mining metals for the Tripods. And in some places, there are hunts."

"Hunts?"

"The Tripods hunt men, as men hunt foxes." I shivered. "And they take men and women into their cities, for reasons at which we can only guess."

"They have cities, then?"

"Not on this side of the sea. I have not seen one, but I know those who have. Towers and spires of metal, it is said, behind a great encircling wall. Gleaming ugly places."

I said, "Do you know how long it has been?"

"That the Tripods have ruled? More than a hundred years. But to the Capped, it is the same as ten thousand." He gave me his hand. "Do your best, Will."

"Yes," I said. His grasp was firm.

"I will hope to meet you again, in the White Mountains."

The next day, as he had said, he was gone. I set about making my preparations. There was a loose stone in the back wall of the den, with a hiding place behind it. Only Jack knew of it, and Jack would not come here again. I put things there—food, a spare shirt, a pair of shoes—ready for my journey. I took the food a little at a time, choosing what would keep best—salt beef and ham, a whole small cheese, oats and such. I think my mother noticed some of the things were missing, and was puzzled.

I was sorry at the thought of leaving her, and my father, and of their unhappiness when they found me gone. The Caps offered no remedy for human grief. But I could not stay, any more than a sheep could walk through a slaughterhouse door, once it knew what lay beyond. And I knew that I would rather die than wear a Cap.

THREE

THE ROAD TO THE SEA

TWO THINGS MADE ME WAIT LONGER THAN A week before I set out. The first was that the moon was new, no more than a sliver of light, and I was reckoning to travel by night. I needed a half-moon at least for that. The other was something I had not expected: Henry's mother died.

She and my mother were sisters. She had been ill for a long time, but her actual death was sudden. My mother took charge of things, and the first thing she did was to bring Henry over to our house and put up a bed for him in my room. This was not welcome, from any point of view, but naturally I could not object to it. My sympathy was coldly offered, and coldly received, and after that we kept to ourselves, as far as was possible for two boys sharing a not very large room.

It was a nuisance, I decided, but not really important. The nights were not yet light enough for me to travel, and I presumed that he would be going back home after the funeral. But when, on the morning of the funeral, I said something of this to my mother, I found to my horror that I was wrong.

She said, "Henry's staying with us."

"For how long?"

"For good. Until you have both been Capped, anyway. Your Uncle Ralph has too much to do on the farm to be able to look after a boy, and he doesn't want to leave him in the care of servants all day."

I did not say anything, but my expression must have been revealing. She said, with unusual sternness, "And I will not have you sulking about it! He has lost his mother, and you should have the decency to show some compassion."

I said, "Can't I have my own room, at least? There's the apple room spare."

"I would have given you your room back, but for the way you've behaved. In less than a year, you will be a man. You must learn to act like a man, not a sullen child."

"But . . ."

"I will not discuss it with you," she said angrily. "If you say another word, I shall speak to your father."

With which she left the room, her skirt sweeping imperiously round the door. Thinking about it, I decided that it made small difference. If I hid my clothes in the mill room, I could sneak out after he was asleep and change there. I was determined to leave, as planned, on the half-moon.

There was heavy rain during the next two days, but after that it cleared, and a blazing hot afternoon dried up most of the mud. Everything went well. Before going to bed, I had hidden my clothes and pack, and a couple of big loaves with them. After that it was only a matter of staying awake, and, keyed up as I was, it did not prove difficult. Eventually Henry's breathing, on the far side of the room, became deep and even in sleep. I lay and thought about the journey: the sea, the strange lands beyond, the Great Lake, and the mountains on which snow lay all summer through. Even without what I had learned of the Tripods and the Caps, the idea was exciting.

The moon rose above the level of my window, and I slipped out of bed. Carefully I opened the bedroom door, and carefully closed it after me. The house was very quiet. The stairs creaked a little under my feet, but no one would pay attention even if they heard it. It was an old wooden house, and creakings at night were not unusual. I went through the big door to the mill room, found my clothes, and dressed quickly. Then out through the door by the river. The wheel was motionless, and the water gurgled and splashed, black streaked with silver, all around it.

Once across the bridge, I felt much safer. In a few minutes I would be clear of the village. A cat tiptoed delicately across the cobbles, and another, on a doorstep, licked its moon-bright fur. A dog barked, hearing me, perhaps, and suspicious, but not near enough to be alarming. With the Widow Ingold's cottage behind me, I broke into a run. I arrived at the den panting and out of breath, but pleased with myself for having got away undetected.

With flint and steel and an oil-soaked rag, I lit a candle, and set about filling my pack. I had over-estimated the amount of space at my disposal; after several reshufflings I still could not get one loaf in. Well, I could carry it for now, and I proposed to stop and eat at dawn. There would be room after that. I had a last look around the den, making sure I had left nothing I would need, doused the candle and slipped it into my pocket, and went out.

It was a good night to be going. The sky bright with stars—all suns, like our own?—and the half-moon rising, the air gentle. I picked up my pack, to put it on. As I did, a voice spoke from the shadows, a few feet away. Henry's voice.

He said, "I heard you go out, and I followed you."

I could not see his face, but I thought there was a mocking tone in his voice. I may have been wrong—it may have been no more than nervousness—but just then I thought he was crowing over having tracked me down. I felt blind anger at this and, dropping my pack, rushed at him. Blind anger was no help. He knocked me down, and I got up, and he knocked me down again. In a short time I was on the ground, and he was sitting on me, pinioning my wrists with his hands. I struggled and sweated and heaved, but it was no good. He had me quite firmly.

"Listen," he said, "I want to tell you something. I know you're running away. You must be, with that pack. What I'm saying is, I want to come with you."

For answer, I made a quick jerk and twist, but his body rolled with mine, and kept me fastened. He said, panting a little, "I want to come with you. There's nothing for me here, now."

His mother, my Aunt Ada, had been a quick, lively, warm-hearted woman, even during the long months of illness. My Uncle Ralph, on the other hand, was a gloomy and taciturn man, who had been willing—perhaps relieved—to let his son go to another's home. I saw what Henry meant.

There was something else, too, of more practical

importance. If I had beaten him in the fight—what then? Leave him here, with the risk of his raising the alarm? There was nothing else I could have done. Whereas if he were to come with me . . . I could give him the slip before we reached the port, and Captain Curtis. I had no intention of taking him there with me. I still disliked him, and even if I had not, I would have been reluctant to share the secrets I had had from Ozymandias.

I had stopped struggling. I said, "Let me up."

"Can I come with you?"

"Yes."

He allowed me to get up. I dusted myself, and we stared at each other in the moonlight. I said, "You haven't brought any food, of course. We'll have to share what I've got."

A couple of days would see us within reach of the port, and I had enough for two for that time.

"Come on," I said. "We'd better get started."

We made good progress through bright moonlight and, when dawn came, were well clear of familiar country. I called a brief halt, and we rested, and ate half of one of the loaves with cheese, and drank water from a stream. Then we continued, more and more tired as the day wore on and the sun scorched its way up through a dry blue sky.

It was about midday and we were hot and sweating when, reaching the crest of a rise, we looked down into a saucer-shaped valley. The land was well-cultivated. There was a village and other dwellings dotted about, with the ant-like figures of men working in the fields. The road ran through the valley and the village. Henry clutched my arm, pointing.

"Look!"

Four men on horseback were making for the village. It could have been any errand. On the other hand, it could have been a search party, looking for us.

I came to a decision. We had been skirting a wood. I said, "We'll stay in the wood till evening. We can get some sleep, and be fresh for the night."

"Do you think traveling by night is the best way?" Henry asked. "I know we're less likely to be seen, but we can't see as well ourselves. We could work around the top of the ridge—there's no one up here."

I said, "You do as you like. I'm lying up."

He shrugged. "We'll stay here, if you say so."

His easy acquiescence did not soothe me. I had the uneasy feeling that what he had said was not unreasonable. I made my way in silence into the wood, and Henry followed. We found a place, deep in the brush, where we were not likely to be noticed even by someone passing quite close, and stretched out. I must have fallen asleep almost at once.

When I awoke, it was nearly dark. I saw Henry asleep beside me. If I were to get up quietly, I might be able to sneak away without waking him. The idea was tempting. It seemed unfair, though, to leave him here, in a wood, with night coming on. I put my hand out to shake him, and noticed something as I did so: he had looped the strap of my pack around his arm, so that I could not have taken it without disturbing him. The possibility had occurred to him, too!

He woke at my touch. We had the rest of the loaf, and a chunk of ham, before moving off. The trees were dense, and we did not see much of the sky until we came out. I realized then that the gloom was not simply due to the near approach of night: it had clouded over while we slept, and I felt an occasional heavy drop of rain on my bare arms and face. The half-moon was not going to be much help behind that cover.

In fading light, we made our way down into the valley, and up the slope beyond. Lamps were lit in the windows of houses, enabling us to give them a wide berth. There was a flurry of rain, but the evening was warm and it dried on us as we walked. At the top we looked down at the clustering lights of the village, and then went on to the southeast. Darkness fell rapidly after that. We were on rolling upland, mainly of close-cropped grass. At one point we came across a ramshackle hut, plainly deserted, and Henry suggested staying there till the light improved, but I would not have it, and he plodded on behind me.

It was some time before either of us spoke. Then Henry said, "Listen."

In some annoyance, I said, "What is it now?"

"I think someone's coming after us."

I heard it myself: the sound of feet on the grass behind us. And more than one pair of feet. We could have been seen by people in the village, warned to watch out for us by the four horsemen. And they could have come up the hill after us, and could now be quietly closing in. I whispered, "Run for it!"

Without waiting for him, I started pelting through the night's blackness. I could hear Henry running nearby, and I thought I could also hear our pursuers. I put on a fresh spurt. As I did, a stone turned under my right foot. There was a jolt of pain and I fell, gasping as the air was forced from my lungs.

Henry had heard my fall. He checked, and said, "Where are you? Are you all right?"

The moment I tried to put weight on my right ankle, I felt sick with pain. Henry tried to lift me, and I groaned in protest.

"Are you hurt?" he asked.

"My ankle . . . I think it's broken. You'd better get on. They'll be here any moment."

He said, in an odd voice, "I think they're here now."

"What?"

There was warm breath on my cheek. I put my hand out and touched something woolly, which immediately backed away.

"Sheep!"

Henry said, "I suppose they were curious. They do that sort of thing sometimes."

"You stupid fool!" I said. "You've had us running from a flock of sheep, and now look what's happened."

He did not say anything, but knelt beside me and started feeling my ankle. I winced, and bit my lip to avoid crying out.

He said, "I don't think it's a break. Probably a sprain, or something. But you'll have to rest up a day or two."

I said savagely, "That sounds fine."

"We'd better get you back to the hut. I'll give you a fireman's lift."

I had felt odd spots of rain again. Now it started coming down heavily—enough to dampen my inclination to reply angrily and refuse his help. He heaved me up on his back. It was a nightmarish journey. He had difficulty getting a proper hold, and I think I was heavier than he had bargained for. He had to keep putting me down and resting. It was pitch black, and the rain was sluicing out of the heavens. Every time he put me down, the pain stabbed my foot. As time went on, I began to think that he had taken the wrong direction and missed the hut in the dark; it would have been easy enough to do so.

But at last it loomed up, out of the night, and the door opened when he lifted the latch. There was a scampering, probably of rats, and he carried me the last few feet and set me down, with a sigh of exhaustion. Stumbling about, he found a pile of straw in a corner, and I crawled over to it. My foot was throbbing, and I was soaked and miserable. Moreover, we had slept much of the previous day. It took me a long time to get to sleep.

When I awoke it was daylight, and the rain had stopped. The deep blue sky of early morning was framed by a glassless window. The hut was furnished only by a bench and a trestle table, with an old saucepan and kettle and a couple of china mugs hanging on hooks against one wall. There was a fireplace with a stack of wood, and the heap of straw that we were lying on. We? Henry was not there: the straw was empty where he had been lying. I called and, after a moment, called again. There was no answer. I dragged myself up, wincing with pain, and edged to the door, hopping and hanging on to the wall.

There was no sign of Henry. Then I saw that the pack was not on the floor, where I had dropped it the night before.

I hobbled out, and sat against the stone wall of the hut. The first horizontal rays of the sun warmed me, while I thought about my situation. Henry, it seemed clear, had abandoned me, and taken the rest of the food with him. After wishing himself on me, he had left me here, helpless and—the more so as I thought about it—hungry. It was no good trying to think clearly. Anger was irresistible, and I found myself wallowing in it. At least it helped me forget my throbbing foot, and the empty void of my stomach.

Even when I was calm enough to start working things out, it did not improve matters much. I was a couple of miles at least from the nearest dwelling. I supposed I could crawl that distance, though it was not likely to be enjoyable. Or perhaps someone—a shepherd, maybe—would come up within hailing distance during the day. Either way it meant being carted back to Wherton in disgrace. Altogether, a miserable and humiliating end to the adventure. I started to feel sorry for myself.

I was at a low point when I heard someone on the far side of the hut and, a moment later, Henry's voice:

"Where are you, Will?"

I answered, and he came around. I said, "I thought you'd pushed off. You took the pack."

"Well, I needed it to carry things."

"What things?"

"It will be a couple of days before you can move. I thought it best to get hold of stuff while I could."

He opened the pack, and showed me a loaf, a hunk of cold roast beef, and a pork pie.

"I got it from a farmhouse down the hill," he said. "The larder window was open. Not a very big one—I thought I'd got stuck at one stage."

I felt immensely relieved, but at the same time resentful. He looked at me, grinning, waiting to be praised for his resourcefulness. I said sharply, "What about the food that was in the pack already?"

Henry stared at me. "I stuck it on the shelf. Didn't you see?"

I hadn't, of course, because I hadn't looked.

It was three days before my ankle was strong enough to travel. We stayed in the hut, and twice more Henry went down into the valley and foraged for food. I had time on my hands: time to think. Henry, it was true, had raised the false alarm over the sheep, but only because he had keener hearing: I had been as much deceived. And it was I who had insisted on traveling by night, with no moon, while he had wanted to lie up. And now I was dependent on him. Misgivings remained—one does not overcome as longstanding a hostility as ours in a few days, especially when under an obligation—but I did not see how I could carry out my plan of losing him before I reached Rumney. In the end, I told him it all—where I was heading, what I had learned from Ozymandias.

He said, "It was because of the Capping that I really wanted to get away. I didn't have any place in mind, of course, but I thought I might be able to hide, for a time at any rate."

I remembered Ozymandias asking me if there was anyone else who might be willing to go south, and my reply. I put my fingers down inside the lining of my jacket.

"This is the map," I said.

FOUR

BEANPOLE

WE CAME INTO RUMNEY IN THE EARLY
evening of a day that had been alternately
bright and stormy; we were wet and tired, and
my ankle was aching. No one paid us any attention.
For one thing, of course, it was a town, and people
in a town did not expect to be able to identify everyone as local or foreigner, as they would in a village.
And this was a port, also—a place of comings and
goings, quite unlike the easy familiar round of the
country. There was an exciting bustle of activity, the
glimpse of sea at the end of a long street, men in
blue jerseys sucking on pipes, a few tardy seagulls

grabbing out of the air for food. And all the smells: tobacco, tar, spices, the smell of the sea itself.

Dusk was thickening by the time we reached the harbor. There were dozens of boats of all sizes tied up, and others standing out in the harbor, sails close-reefed on their masts. We wandered along the quay, reading their names. The *Maybelle*, the *Black Swan*, *Venturer*, the *Gay Gordon*—but no *Orion*.

"She might be at sea," I said.

"What do you think we should do?"

"We'll have to find somewhere to sleep."

Henry said, "I wouldn't mind finding some food, as well."

We had finished our provisions that morning. The windows of the taverns along the front were brightly lit in the twilight, and we could hear singing from some of them. From some, also, issued rich cooking smells that made my belly groan in protest against its emptiness. In a nearby window there was a board, and chalked on it: HOT PIES—SIXPENCE. I still had a little money, which I had brought with me, and which I had not dared spend before. I told Henry to wait for me, and slipped in through the door.

It was a low-ceilinged, wooden-beamed room, with scrubbed deal tables at which people were eating, swilling the food down with mugs of beer. I did not study them closely, but went to the serving counter, where I handed over my shilling and took the two pies from a dark girl who was talking all the time to a sailor at the nearest table. I made for the door with them, but a hand reached out and took a crushing grip on my arm.

He looked a very big man, too, until he stood up. I saw then that he was thick-set but, because of the shortness of his legs, only a couple of inches taller than I. He had a yellow beard, and yellow hair receding from his forehead, where the wires of his Cap showed up. He said, in a harsh, barking voice, "Well, lad, how would you like to be a sailor?"

I shook my head. "No."

He stared at me. "Are you from these parts?"

"Yes."

"Would you say your folks will be seeking you if you don't come back tonight?"

I said boldly, "I only live three streets from here. They'll be looking for me if I'm not back right away."

He was silent for a second and then laughed, deeply and unpleasantly.

"You tell me so, with an accent like that! You're from the country if ever I heard a country lad." I gave a quick twist, and tried to break free. "Now then, no trouble. Save your strength for the *Black Swan*."

He dragged me to the door. No one paid any attention, and I realized the scene could not be an uncommon one. Crying out would do no good, either. If they did not ignore me, they could very well ask questions which I did not want to answer. There might be a chance of breaking clear outside. Not much, though, because I had felt his strength. And the *Black Swan* was moored no more than a hundred yards away.

I saw him as we reached the door: a tall man, with a long, thin-lipped face, black-bearded and swarthy. I called out:

"Captain Curtis!"

He gave me one swift glance, and challenged my captor.

"Leave him be, Rowley. That's my boy. I signed him on this afternoon."

The man he had called Rowley looked for a moment as though he were going to argue, but Captain Curtis took a step toward him, and he let go of my arm. He said, "You should keep him on board, and not let him go wandering around the town."

"I can look after my own crew," Captain Curtis said. "I want no advice from you."

Ozymandias had said that crossing the sea would be the easiest part, and he was right. The *Orion* was one of the ships out in the harbor—we had nearly missed her, because she was sailing on the midnight tide— and Captain Curtis took us to her in a dinghy. He single-oared us across the harbor, threading his way between lines and buoys, to the ship's dark hulk. She was a trawler, of no more than a hundred tons, but she looked enormous as I made my way, swaying and barking my knuckles, up the rope ladder to the deck. Only one of the crew of six was on board, a tall, awkward, gently spoken man with gold rings in his ears. The others were Capped, Captain Curtis said, but he was one of us.

It was essential that we should not be seen by the

rest of the crew, because of the difficulty of explaining our one-way voyage. We were put in Captain Curtis's own cabin, where there were two bunks. It did not occur to us to ask where he was going to sleep. We were both tired. I fell asleep at once, and was only half-wakened, some time later, by the pounding of feet overhead, and the grinding roar of the anchor chain coming up.

I had heard tales of the motion of the waves making people sick, but though the *Orion* was rolling a little when I awoke the next morning, it was not enough to trouble me. The Captain brought us breakfast: bacon, fried eggs, a hillock of fried potatoes, and mugs full of a hot brown liquid that gave off a strange but glorious smell. Henry sniffed at his.

"What is it?"

"Coffee. It comes from a long way off, and costs a lot to landsmen. Are you all right?" We nodded. "No one will come in here. They know my door is always locked. But keep quiet, all the same. It's only for today. With this wind we shall be in harbor before sundown."

The cabin had a porthole, through which we could stare out at blue waves, topped here and there with white. It was a strange sight for two who had never seen a stretch of water bigger than the lake up at the Manor House, and at first we were fascinated, but soon grew used to it, and at last bored. During the day, only one thing happened to break the monotony, though that was startling enough.

In the middle of the afternoon, above the creak of ropes and stays and the slap of the waves, we heard a new sound, a high-pitched wailing, far off, that seemed to rise up from the sea itself. Henry was at the porthole. He said, "Come and look, Will."

There was urgency in his voice. I put down the piece of wood I had been trying to whittle into the shape of a boat, and went to join him. The sea was blue-green and empty, marked only by the silver bar of sunlight that shimmered out to the horizon. But something moved in the silver, a flicker in the bright haze. Until, crossing from the sun-path into the blue, it took on shape. A Tripod, followed by a second, and a third. Six of them all told.

I said, in wonder, "Can they walk on water?"

"They're coming this way."

They were moving fast. I saw that their legs did not move, as they did in crossing land, but remained fixed and triangulated, and that each foot raised a bow-wave which, supposing they were of the usual size, must be twenty feet high. They were traveling much faster than a horse gallops. They kept their course toward us, their speed seeming to increase as the bow-waves rose higher above the line of the horizon. Each foot, I saw, ended in a kind of float. And they were on a collision course with the *Orion*. If one of them hit her, and capsized her—what chance would we have, below decks, locked in a cabin?

At about twenty-five yards' distance, the leading Tripod veered sharply left to cut across our stern. The rest followed. There was a howling like a dozen different winds, running up and down the scale. Then the first of the waves hit the ship, and she tossed like a cork. We both fell, as the cabin heaved under us, and I banged myself painfully against the stanchion of the bunk. I started to get up, and was flung toward the open porthole, as the *Orion* rolled. The sea came up to meet me. A wave splashed in, drenching both of us. And the howling was increasing again as the Tripods came around in another circuit of the ship.

They made three or four—I was not in a mood for keeping strict count—before continuing on their way. Captain Curtis told us later that this sort of encounter was not uncommon; the *Orion* had had half a dozen previously. No one knew why they did it—as a joke, perhaps. It was a joke that could have a grim ending: quite a few boats had foundered as a result. We were merely soaked and shaken. I think I was more shaken by their appearance than their actions. They dominated sea, as well as land. If I had thought about it, I suppose, I would have assumed that. But I had not, and the reality depressed me.

Henry said to the Captain, "They didn't sound like Tripods."

"Sound? I suppose you've only heard the Capping Call. North of the Channel they see to the Cappings, and that's about all. In the south you will see more of them, and hear them. They have all kinds of calls."

That was another thing. I had thought of them in connection with the Cappings, and only that.

What Ozymandias had said about hunting men as men hunted foxes had not really affected me. My mind had rejected the idea as fantasy. It did so no longer. I was depressed. I was also quite a bit scared.

Captain Curtis took us off the *Orion* in much the same manner as he had brought us on board. He gave us food before we left, filling my pack, and providing Henry with another. He also gave us last-minute advice.

"Keep under cover, avoid all contact with the people. They speak a different language, remember. You won't understand them, and they won't understand you. If they pick you up, they will hand you over for Capping."

He looked at us, lamplight catching deep rusty gold among the blackness of his whiskers. His was a hard face, until one got to know it.

"It's happened before. With lads like yourselves, heading for the mountains, or with lads who have run away from someone like Rowley. They've been taken by foreigners, and Capped in a foreign land. They all became Vagrants, and bad ones at that.

"Perhaps it's because the machines are set for thoughts in that language, and not being able to understand them cripples you. Or perhaps they just go on until either they get a response or break you— and you don't know how to respond the way they want. Anyway, keep clear of people. Get out of this town fast, and stay away from towns and villages after that."

He brought the dinghy up to a careening hard. Two or three boats lay on their sides, but there was no sign of life. One could hear distant noises— someone hammering, voices faintly singing—but close at hand there were only the hulks of boats, hard-edged in moonlight, the low line of the harbor wall, and the roofs of the town beyond. A strange town, in a strange land, whose people we could not, and must not, speak to. The dinghy's keel grated on pebbles.

"Off you go," Captain Curtis whispered. "Good luck!"

The pebbles under our feet made a crunching sound that was loud in the quiet night, and we stood for a moment, listening. Nothing moved. I looked back, and saw the dinghy disappear behind a larger boat, moored close in. We were on our own. I gestured to Henry, and set off up the hard. One came out on the front, Captain Curtis had said, turned left, walked a hundred yards, and there was a road to the right. Following it would take us out of town. A quarter of an hour, and we could relax our vigilance, if only slightly.

What we had, though, was something like a quarter of a minute.

A road ran alongside the harbor wall and on the far side of it there was a row of houses, taller and seemingly narrower than those in Rumney. As Henry and I moved across the entrance to the hard, a door opened across the way, and a man came out. Apparently seeing us, he yelled. We ran, and he ran after us, and others spilled out from the open door. I made perhaps fifty yards along the front, before I was caught and held. The one who had grabbed me, a big, wild-looking man whose breath smelled unpleasant, shook me and demanded something: at least, I could tell that he was asking a question. I looked for Henry, and saw that they had caught him, too. I wondered if Captain Curtis had heard anything of the disturbance. Probably not, and if he had there was nothing he could do. He had told us that plainly.

They dragged us across the road. The house was a tavern, but not much like the tavern in Rumney. We were in a small room, full of tobacco smoke and smelling of liquor, but both tobacco and liquor smelled differently. There was a bar counter, and half a dozen marble-topped tables, with high-backed chairs. The men stood around us, talking incomprehensibly and making a lot of gestures with their hands. I had a feeling they were disappointed about something. At the back of the room there was a staircase which turned on itself, leading both upstairs and down. Someone was watching us from the upper stairs, gazing over the heads that surrounded us.

Although he was tall and had a face that seemed old enough, he had not been Capped. But the striking thing about him was what he wore on his face. Pieces of thin metal ran from behind his ears to hold a frame with a couple of round pieces of glass, one in front of each eye. One of them was somewhat larger than the other, giving him a peculiar cockeyed look. Even in our present predicament, I thought him funny. He looked odd enough, in fact, to be a Vagrant, though that was impossible since he was not yet Capped. It dawned on me that the apparent oldness of his face was the result of this contraption he wore. His features behind it were thin. He was a lot taller than I, but he could be near my age.

But I did not have much opportunity for speculation. After some minutes of badgering us in their strange language, the men plainly reached a conclusion. There was shrugging and waggling of hands, and we were shoved toward the stairs. They took us down, and pushed us through a door at the bottom. I fell sprawling from a blow, and heard a key turn in the lock behind us.

For half an hour or so we heard sounds of people moving about over our heads, and a low grumble of voices. Then there were noises of departure, and through the small, vertically barred window, high on one wall, we saw legs outlined against the moonlight as those who had been drinking went home. No one came down to us. We heard bolts slammed, the stamping of a last pair of feet—that would be the landlord—and after that nothing but a distant scratching that was probably a rat.

The most likely thing was that we were being held for a Capping. I was scared again, realizing how close this might be—it could be tomorrow, even—and, for the first time it seemed, envisioning the lonely mad life ahead. There would not even be Henry, because Vagrants wandered apart, each cloaked in his own wild dreams and fancies.

Henry said, "I wonder . . ."

Hearing his voice was a small relief. I said, "What?"

"The window. If I gave you a leg up . . ."

I did not believe they would have imprisoned us in a place we could break out of so easily, but it was something to do. Henry knelt by the wall, and I stood on his shoulders in my stockinged feet. There was a twinge of pain in my ankle, but I disregarded it. He raised up slowly, while I kept my hands against the wall and reached for the window bars. I got hold at last, first of one and then another. I heaved and pushed, but they were firmly bedded in stone, top and bottom. Henry shifted under me, and I called down:

"It's no good."

"Try again. If you . . ."

He broke off, and I heard what he had heard: the scrape of a key against the sides of the lock. I jumped down, and stood watching the darker rectangle of the door. Slowly it creaked open. There was light beyond, a lamp held up, and the light gleamed on small circles of glass. It was the boy who had watched us from the stairs.

Then he spoke and, to my greater astonishment, in English.

"Do not make a noise," he said. "I will help you."

Silently we followed him up the stairs, the old timbers creaking under us, and across the bar room. He drew the bolts very carefully, but they sounded hideously loud. At last the door was open. I whispered, "Thank you. We . . ."

He thrust his head forward, the contraption on his nose looking even more ludicrous, and said, "You wish to go to the boat? I can still help."

"Not to a boat. South."

"South? From the town, into land? Not to the sea?"

"Yes," I said, "inland."

"I can help there also." He blew out the lamp, and set it down inside the door. "I will show you."

The moonlight was still bright on the waterfront and the gently bobbing masts of the boats in the harbor, but in places the stars were hidden by cloud, and a breeze was getting up from the sea. He started along the way Captain Curtis had said, but before long led us into an alley. We went up steps, and the alley twisted and turned. It was so narrow that moonlight did not penetrate; there was barely enough light to see our way.

Later there was a road, then another alley, and a road again. The road widened, houses thinned on either side, and at last we reached a place where there was a bright meadow, dotted with the dark shapes of cows. He stopped beside a grassy bank.

"This goes south," he said.

I said, "Will you get into trouble? Will they know it was you that let us out?"

He shrugged, his head bobbing. "It does not

matter." He said it like "mat-air." "Will you tell me why you wish to go into land?" He corrected himself: "In-land?"

I hesitated only for a moment. "We have heard of a place, in the south, where there are no Cappings, and no Tripods."

"Cappings?" he repeated. "Tripods?" He touched his head, and said a word in his own language. "The great ones, with three legs—they are Tripods? A place without them? Is it possible? Everyone puts on—the Cap?—and the Tripods go everywhere."

"Perhaps not in the mountains."

He nodded. "And there are mountains in the south. Where one could hide, if no more. Is that where you go? Is it possible that I can come?"

I looked at Henry, but it scarcely needed confirmation. Someone whom we already knew to be resourceful, who knew the country and the language. It was almost too good to be true.

"Can you come as you are?" I asked him. "Going back would be risky."

"I am ready now." He put a hand out, first to me and then to Henry. "My name—I am Zhan-pole."

He looked odd and solemn standing there, tall and thin, with that strange metal-and-glass thing on his face. Henry laughed.

"More like Beanpole!"

He stared at Henry inquiringly for a moment. Then he laughed, too.

FIVE

THE CITY OF THE ANCIENTS

W E TRAMPED THROUGH THE NIGHT, COVER-
ing ten or twelve miles before, with the summer dawn edging over the horizon, we **broke**
off, to rest and eat. While we rested, Beanpole told
us the reason for the men rushing out from the tavern to catch us the previous night: some of the local
boys had been damaging the boats on the hard, and
the sailors thought we were the culprits. A stroke of
bad luck, though it had turned out well. He told us
. something about himself also. His parents had died
when he was a baby; and his uncle and aunt owned
the tavern. They seemed to have looked after him all

right, but in a distant way, with not much affection or, at any rate, not much shown. I got the impression that they may even have been a little scared of him. This is not as silly as it sounds because there was one thing that stood out about him: he had quite a tremendous brain.

His speaking English, for instance: he had found an old book, giving instructions in the language, and taught himself. And the contraption on his face. His eyesight was poor, and he had worked it out that, since mariners' telescopes helped sailors to see at a distance, a glass in front of each eye might enable him to see more clearly. He had messed about with lenses until he found some that did. There were other things he had tried, with less success, but you could see how they might have worked. He had noticed that hot air rises, and had filled a pig's bladder with steam from a kettle and seen it go up to the ceiling. So he had tried making a big balloon out of oilskin and fixing it to a platform with a brazier under the opening, hoping it would rise into the sky; but nothing happened. Another idea that had not worked out had been for putting springs on the ends of stilts—he had broken a leg the previous year trying that one out.

Lately he had been more and more uneasy about the prospect of being Capped, rightly guessing that it would put an end to his inventing things. I realized that it was not just Jack, and myself, and Henry, who had doubts about Capping. Probably everyone, or almost everyone, felt like that, but because adults were all on the side of the Tripods dared not say so. Beanpole said his balloon idea had come from this: a thought of himself drifting through the sky to strange lands, perhaps somewhere finding one where there were no Tripods. He had been interested in us because he had guessed we came from north of the sea, and there were stories that the Tripods were fewer there.

We came to a crossroads not long after restarting our journey, and I was once more made aware of our luck in finding him. I would have taken the road south, but he chose west.

"Because of the . . ." What he said sounded like "Shmand-Fair." "I do not know your name for it."

"What is it?" Henry asked.

"It is too hard to explain, I think. You will see."

· · ·

The Shmand-Fair started inside a town, but we skirted it and reached a small hill, topped with ruins, on the southern edge. Looking down we could see a track, on which were two parallel straight lines, gleaming in the sunshine, which ran from the town and disappeared in the far distance. The town end had an open space, where half a dozen objects looking like great boxes on wheels were linked together. As we watched, a dozen horses were harnessed in pairs and yoked to the nearest of the boxes. A man was mounted on the lead pair, and another on the second pair from the box. At a signal, the horses strained forward and the boxes began to move, slowly and then faster. When they were going quite fast, the eight horses in front broke free, and galloped obliquely away. The remaining four continued pulling the boxes on and past our vantage point. There were five boxes altogether. The two in front had openings in their sides, and we could see people sitting in them; the rest were closed.

Beanpole explained that twelve horses were needed to start the wheels rolling along the lines, but once they were moving four were enough. The Shmand-Fair took goods and people south for a long way—more than a hundred miles, it was said. It would save us a lot of walking. I agreed, but asked how we were going to get aboard, since the horses had been going at full tilt when it passed us. He had an answer for that, too. Although the ground on which the lines were laid looked level, there were parts with slopes up or down. On the down slopes, the horseman could brake the wheels of the boxes. In the case of up gradients, the horses had to pull against the drag, which sometimes reduced them almost to walking pace before they reached the top.

We followed the now empty lines away from the town. They were of iron, their tops polished to brightness by the wheels, and were fastened on massive planks, whose surface showed in places through a covering of earth. It was a clever means of travel, but Beanpole was not satisfied with it.

"Steam," he said, musing. "It rises. Also, it pushes. You have seen the lid pushed up from the saucepan? If one made a lot of steam—like a very big kettle—and pushed the carriages from behind? But, no. That is impossible."

We laughed, agreeing. Henry said, "It would be like lifting yourself by pulling on the laces of your shoes."

Beanpole shook his head. "There is a way, I am sure."

Finding the best place for getting on the Shmand-Fair proved easier than I had expected. The gradient was scarcely noticeable, but the crest of the rise was marked by a wooden post, with arms on either side pointing down. There were bushes nearby, which provided cover. We had a wait of half an hour before the next one came in sight, but that was going the wrong way. (I wondered about there being only the one set of tracks, and found later that there were places where the tracks were doubled, so that two could pass.) Eventually, the right one appeared; we saw the horses drop from gallop to canter, and at last to a straining, heaving walk. When the carriages with people had passed, we darted out, and swung aboard the one at the end. Beanpole led the way, clambering up the side and on to the flat top. No sooner had Henry and I followed suit than the Shmand-Fair ground to a halt.

I thought perhaps our extra weight had stopped it, but Beanpole shook his head. He whispered back:

"They have reached the top. The horses rest, and are given water. Then they go on."

And after a five-minute break, they did, quickly gathering speed. There was a bar along the top to hold, and the motion was not unpleasant—better than traveling in a carriage on an ordinary road where one hit boulders and potholes all the time. Henry and I looked out at the landscape, as it flashed past. Beanpole stared at the sky. I suspected he was still pondering his idea of using steam instead of horses. It was a pity, I thought, that with so many ideas in his head he could not learn to tell the difference between sensible and ridiculous ones.

From time to time there were halts in villages, and people got on and off and goods were loaded and unloaded. We lay flat, and kept silent, hoping no one would come up on top. Once a large millstone was unloaded, with a lot of panting and cursing, from directly beneath us, and I recalled what difficulty my father had found in getting a new millstone up to Wherton. There was a raised bank, not far from the village, which ran straight for miles, and it occurred to me that Shmand-Fair could be built along that. Or perhaps had been built, long ago, before the Tripods? The thought, like so many others recently, was startling.

Twice we saw Tripods in the distance. It struck me that, being more numerous in this country, they must do a great deal of damage to crops. Not only crops, Beanpole said. Animals were often killed by the great metal feet; and people, too, if they were not quick enough to get out of the way. This, like everything else, was taken for granted. But no longer by us; having started asking questions, each doubt set loose a score of others.

Toward evening, during a halt to refresh the horses, we saw a town in the distance. It looked bigger than the town from which the Shmand-Fair had started, and Beanpole thought it might be the place where it ended. It seemed a good opportunity to take our leave, and we did so when the horses began to move again to the cries of the horseman. We slipped off as the Shmand-Fair gathered speed, and watched the carriages roll away. We had been traveling almost continuously southeast, a distance of anything from fifty to a hundred miles. Less than a hundred, though, or we ought to have seen what was shown as a landmark on the map: the ruins of one of the great-cities of the ancients. The thing to do, we agreed, was head south.

We traveled on while the light held. It was warm still, but clouds had come up. We looked for shelter before darkness halted us, but could find nothing, and settled at last for a dry ditch. Fortunately, it did not rain during the night. In the morning, clouds still threatened, but no more than that, and we had a snack of bread and cheese and continued on our way. We went up a rise, beside a wood, which would offer cover if there were a risk of being seen. Henry reached the top first, and stood there, stock still and staring ahead. I quickened my step, anxious to see what he was gazing at. When I reached him, I, too, stopped in wonder.

• • •

It was the ruins of the great-city which lay ahead of us, a mile or two distant. I had never seen anything remotely like it before. It stretched for miles, rising in hills and valleys. The forest had invaded it—there was the tossing green of trees everywhere—but everywhere also were the gray and white and yellow bones of buildings. The trees followed lines among them, like veins in some monstrous creature.

We stood in silence, until Beanpole murmured, "My people built that."

Henry said, "How many lived there, do you think? Thousands? Hundreds of thousands? A million?"

I said, "We shall have to go a long way around. I can see no end."

"Around?" Beanpole asked. "But why? Why not through?"

I remembered Jack, and his story of the huge ship in the harbor of the great-city south of Winchester. It had not occurred to either of us that he might have done more than gaze from a distance; no one ever approached the great-cities. But that was the way of thinking that came from the Tripods, and the

Caps. Beanpole's suggestion was frightening, and then exciting. Henry said, in a low voice, "Do you think we could get through?"

"We can try," Beanpole said. "If it is too difficult, we can return."

The nature of the veins became clear as we approached. The trees followed the old streets, sprouting out of the black stone of which they had been built, and thrusting their tops up above the canyons formed by the buildings on either side. We walked in their dark cool shade, at first in silence. I did not know about the others, but I needed all the courage I could summon up. Birds sang above our heads, emphasizing the quietness and gloom of the depths through which we made our way. Only gradually did we start taking an interest in our surroundings, and talking—at the beginning in whispers and then more naturally.

There were strange things to be seen. Signs of death, of course—the white gleam of bone that had once borne flesh. We had expected that. But one of the first skeletons we saw was slumped inside a rusted oblong, humped in the middle, which rested on metal wheels, rimmed with a hard black substance. There were other similar contraptions, and Beanpole stopped by one and peered inside. He said, "Places for men to sit. And wheels. So, a carriage of some nature."

Henry said, "It can't be. There's nowhere to harness the horse. Unless the shafts rusted away."

"No," Beanpole said. "They are all the same. Look."

I said, "Perhaps they were huts, for people to rest in when they were tired of walking."

"With wheels?" Beanpole asked. "No. They were carriages without horses. I am sure."

"Pushed by one of your big kettles, maybe!" Henry said.

Beanpole stared at it. He said, quite seriously, "Perhaps you are right."

Some of the buildings had fallen down, from age and weathering, and in places many—whole rows sometimes—had been flattened, crushed, it seemed, by a hammer from the sky. But a great number were more or less intact, and eventually we ventured inside one. It had been a shop, plainly, but of enormous size. There were tins everywhere, some still piled on shelves, but most of them scattered on the floor. I picked one up. It had paper around it, with a faded picture of plums. Other tins had pictures, too—fruit, vegetables, bowls of soup. They had held food. It was reasonable enough: with so many people living together, and no land to till, food would have had to be brought to them in containers, just as my mother bottled things in summer for winter use. The tins had rusted, in some places right through, showing a dried-up indistinguishable mess inside.

There were thousands of shops, and we looked in many of them. Their contents amazed us. Great bolts of mildewed cloth, still showing weird colors and patterns; row on row of crumbling cardboard boxes, full of rotting leather shoes; musical instruments, a few familiar but most incredibly weird; figures of women, made from a strange hard substance, clothed in the tattered remnants of dresses. And a place full of bottles, which Beanpole told us was wine. He broke the top off one, and we tasted it but pulled faces at the sourness: it had gone bad long ago. We picked up some things and took them with us: a knife, a small axe with an edge that was rusted but could be sharpened, a kind of flask made of translucent blue material, very light in weight, which would carry water better than the flasks Henry and I had got from Captain Curtis, candles . . . things like that.

But the shop that filled me with awe was quite small. It was tucked away between two much bigger ones, and as well as the usual broken glass it had a barrier of warped and rusted metal in front of it. When I looked in, it was like Aladdin's cave. There were gold rings, set with diamonds and other stones, brooches, necklaces, bangles. And perhaps a score of Watches!

I picked one out. It was gold, too, and had a heavy gold bracelet, which expanded when I put my fingers inside and stretched them; so that it would be made large enough to go over your hand and would then lie snug on your wrist. Or on a thicker wrist than mine. It was loose when I put it on, so I pushed it higher up my arm. It would not go, of course, but it was a Watch. The other two were exploring on the other side of the street. I thought of calling them, and then decided against it.

It was not just that I did not want them to have a Watch like mine, though that was part of it. There was also the memory of my struggle with Henry over my father's Watch, when Jack had helped me to get it off him. And this, I think, was sparked by something less definite, a feeling of discontent. My dislike for Henry had been thrust into the background by the difficulties and dangers which we encountered together and shared. When Beanpole joined us, I had talked to him more, and he had responded: Henry, to some extent, had been left out of things. I had realized this and, I am afraid, been complacent about it.

Today, though, particularly since we had come into the great-city, I had become aware of a change. It was nothing clearcut; just that Henry talked more to Beanpole, that Beanpole directed more of his own remarks to Henry—that there had been a shift, in fact, from it being a matter of Beanpole and myself, with Henry a little bit out of things, to a situation in which I was, to some extent, the excluded one. So it had happened that I had found this shop, with the jewels and the Watches, having left them discussing a strange machine they had found which had four rows of small white buttons with letters on, in front. I looked at the Watch again. No, I was not going to call them.

Eventually, we more or less gave up looking in the shops. In part, this was because our curiosity was sated, but more because we had been several hours in the city. with no sign of approaching the other side. The reverse, in fact. At one point, where devastation had left a great mound of rubble, we climbed up through the bushes and grass that covered it and found ourselves looking down on the waving green and crumbling stone. It stretched about us, seemingly endless, like a sea ribbed with reefs of rock. But for the compass we would have been lost, for the day had clouded and there was no sun to give us direction. As it was, we knew we were still heading south, and the day was less than half-run, but we felt the need to push on faster than we had been doing so far.

We came to wider streets, flanked by bigger buildings, that ran broad and straight for immense distances. We stopped to eat where several of these met; there was a place where the trees had not found a purchase, and we sat chewing our meat and the hard biscuits Captain Curtis had given us—our bread was all gone—on a mossy stone. Afterward, we rested, but Beanpole got up after a while and wandered off. Henry followed him. I lay flat, looking up at the gray sky, and did not answer at first when they called me. But Beanpole called again, and sounded excited. They seemed to have found something interesting.

It was a large hole, surrounded on three sides by rusted rails with steps leading down into the darkness. At the top, opposite the entrance, there was a metal plate which said METRO.

Beanpole said, "The steps—they are so wide that ten people can go side by side. Where do they lead?"

I said, "Does it matter? If we aren't resting, we'd better be getting on."

"If I could see . . ." Beanpole said. "Why was such a thing built, so great a tunnel?"

"Who cares?" I shrugged. "You wouldn't see anything down there."

"We've got candles," Henry said.

I said angrily, "We haven't got time. We don't want to have to spend a night here."

They ignored me. Henry said to Beanpole, "We could go a bit of the way down, and see what there is." Beanpole nodded.

I said, "It's stupid!"

Henry said, "You don't need to come, if you don't want to. You can stay here and rest."

He said it indifferently, already rummaging in his pack for the candles. They would have to be lit, and I was the only one with a tinderbox. But they were determined, I realized, and I might as well give in with as good a grace as I could manage. I said:

"I'll come with you. I still think it's pointless, though."

The stairs descended first into a cavern, which we explored as well as the meager light of the candles permitted. Being less subject to the elements, things had deteriorated less here than in the world above. There were queer machines, showing patches of rust but otherwise undamaged, and a kind of hut with glass in the windows, intact.

And there were tunnels leading off the cavern; some, like the one by which we had entered, with stairs going up, others leading still farther down. Beanpole was all for exploring one of these, and got his way for want of opposition. The steps went a very long way, and at the bottom there was another small tunnel going to the right. Whatever slight interest I had had was gone by now—all I wanted was to get back up into the daylight. But I was not going to suggest this. I had an idea, from the increasing lack of enthusiasm in his replies to Beanpole's comments, that Henry was no more keen than I was on going farther—perhaps less. I reckoned I could leave it to him to call a halt before Beanpole went too far.

Beanpole led the way along the small tunnel, which twisted and ended in a gate of heavy iron bars. It creaked as he pushed it open. We followed him through, and stared at what we could now see.

It was yet another tunnel, but far bigger than the others. We stood on level stone and the tunnel curved up over our heads and went on, beyond the limits of our light. What amazed us, though, was the thing that stood there. I thought at first it was a house, a long low narrow house of glass and metal, and wondered who would have chosen to live here, deep in the earth. Then I saw that it stood in a wide ditch running alongside our level, that there were wheels under it, and that the wheels rested on long metal bars. It was a kind of Shmand-Fair.

But to travel where? Could this tunnel run for a hundred miles, as the track of the Shmand-Fair had done—but underground? To a buried city, perhaps, whose wonders were even greater than those of the city above us? And how? We walked along, and found that carriage was joined to long carriage: four, five, six, we counted, and a little way past the last carriage was the mouth of a smaller tunnel, and the empty lines ran into it and were lost.

The last carriage ended with windows looking ahead. Inside, there was a seat, levers, instruments. I said, "No place to attach the horses. And who would have horses pulling underground?"

Henry said, "They must have used your steam-kettle."

Beanpole was staring greedily at the strange instruments.

"Or a thing more wonderful," he said.

On the way back, we looked inside the carriages; parts of their sides were open, so that one could step into them. There were seats, but a clutter of other things, as well, including heaps of tins of food, such as we had found in the shops, but unrusted—the air down here was cool and dry, as it must be all the time. Other things we could not understand—a rack full of wooden things ending in iron cylinders, for instance. They had small half-hoops of iron on one side with a little iron finger inside. The finger moved when you pressed it; but nothing happened.

"So they carried goods," Beanpole said. "And people, since there are seats."

Henry said, "What are these?"

It was a wooden box, full of what looked like large metal eggs—as big as goose eggs. He picked one out, and showed it to Beanpole. It was made of iron, its surface grooved into squares, and there was a ring at one end. Henry pulled it, and it came away.

Beanpole said, "Can I look?"

Henry handed the egg to him, but clumsily. It fell before Beanpole could grasp it, dropped to the floor, and rolled. It went over the edge of the floor and dropped into the ditch beneath. Henry was going after it, but Beanpole caught his arm.

"Leave it. There are others."

He was bending down toward the box when it happened. There was a tremendous bang under our feet, and the great steel carriage shuddered with the violence of it. I had to clutch an upright pillar to prevent myself being thrown to the ground. Echoes of the bang reverberated along the tunnel, like diminishing hammer blows. Henry said shakily, "What was that?"

But he did not really need telling. Beanpole had dropped his candle, and it had gone out. He put it to Henry's, to relight it. I said:

"If it had not rolled down below the carriage . . ."

There was no need to fill in details. Beanpole said,

"Like fireworks, but more powerful. What would the ancients use such things for?"

He picked up another egg. Henry said,

"I shouldn't mess about with them."

I agreed, though I said nothing. Beanpole handed

Henry his candle, so that he could look at the egg more carefully.

Henry said, "If it goes off . . ."

"They did not go off before," Beanpole said. "They were brought here. I do not think touching will do anything. The ring . . ." He put his finger into it. "You pulled it out, and it fell, and then, a little later . . ."

Before I properly understood what he was doing, he wrenched the ring from the egg. We both cried out, but he ignored us, walked to the opening, and threw the egg under the carriage.

This time, together with the explosion, there was a shattering of glass, and a gust of air blew out my candle. I said angrily, "That was a stupid thing to do!"

"The floor protects us," Beanpole said. "It is not much risk, I think."

"We could have been cut by flying glass."

"I do not think so."

The point was, as I ought to have realized earlier, Beanpole was only sensible as long as his curiosity was not deeply aroused; when something interested him, he had no thought for hazards. Henry said, "I wouldn't do it again, all the same."

He obviously shared my feelings about the experiment. Beanpole said, "It is not necessary. We know how it works. I counted seven after the ring came out."

It was nice to feel I was part of the majority again, even though the other part was Henry. I said, "All right—so you know how it works. What good does that do?"

Beanpole did not reply. He had found himself a pack in one of the shops—the leather was green and moldy but cleaned up fairly well—and he was now taking eggs from the box and putting them inside. I said:

"You're not taking those with you, are you?"

He nodded. "They will be useful, perhaps."

"For what?"

"I do not know. But something."

I said flatly, "You can't. It's not safe for us, either."

"There is no danger unless the ring is pulled."

He had put four in his pack. I looked toward

Henry, to back me up. But he said, "I suppose they might come in handy." He picked one up, and hefted it in his hand. "They're heavy. I think I'll take a couple, though."

I did not know whether he was saying this because he really meant it, or to spite me. It did not make much difference, I thought bitterly. I was back in the minority.

We made our way up through the tunnels, and I was very glad to see the sky, even though it was a still darker gray, with clouds lower and more menacing. Not long afterward, our way was barred by a river, running clear and swift between high banks. There had been many great bridges spanning it, but those we could see had been partly or altogether destroyed; the one directly before us was marked only by half a dozen piles of rubble with the water boiling around them. With nothing to choose between the alternatives, we followed the river to the east.

Four bridges proved hopeless, and then the river forked. It seemed to me that this meant that, if we continued toward the east, we should have to find bridges intact over both branches, doubling the difficulty; and that our best course was to go back and try in the opposite direction. But Henry was opposed to turning back, and Beanpole supported him. There was nothing I could do but tag along resentfully.

My resentment was not diminished by the fact that the very next bridge was intact enough to cross, though the parapet had completely gone at one side, and in the middle the bridge itself had a hole bitten out of the edge which we had to skirt warily. On the far side there were relatively few trees, and the buildings were massive. Then we came to an open space and saw at the end of it a building which, even in ruins, had a magnificence that compelled the eye.

There had been twin towers in front, but one of these had been sliced down the side. On them, and on the whole facade, were carvings in stone, and from roofs and angles stone figures of monstrous animals probed the quiet air. It was a cathedral, I guessed, and it looked bigger even than the great cathedral in Winchester, which I had always believed was the biggest building in the world. The huge wooden door stood open, tilted on its hinges and rotting. Part of the roof of the nave had fallen in, and one could see up past the pillars and buttresses to the sky. We did not go inside: I think none of us wanted to disturb its crumbling silence.

The next thing we discovered was that we had not, in fact, crossed to the opposite bank of the river, but were on an island. The waters which had divided to the west came together again in the east. We had to trail back across the bridge. I was not sorry to see Henry discomfited, but I was too tired to think it worth the extra effort.

It was at this time that Beanpole said to me, "What is it on your arm?"

The Watch had slipped down, without my noticing it, to my wrist. I had to show it to them. Henry looked at it with envy, though he said nothing. Beanpole showed a more dispassionate interest. He said, "I have seen clocks, of course, but not one of these. How is it made to go?"

"You turn the button on the side," I said. "But I did not bother to do that, since it must be so old."

"But it is going."

Disbelievingly, I looked myself. Above the hour

and minute hands, a third, more slender pointer was going around, sweeping the dial. I held the Watch to my ear: it was ticking. I noticed a word on the face: Automatique. It seemed like magic, but could not be. It was another wonder of the ancients.

We all stared at it. Beanpole said, "These trees— some are a hundred years old, I think. And yet it works. What craftsmen they were."

We got across the river at last, half a mile farther up. There was no sign of the city coming to an end; its vastness, which had first awed, and then aroused wonder and curiosity, was now exhausting. We passed many large buildings, including one larger than the cathedral—a side had fallen in and one could see that it was a shop, or a series of shops, right up to the roof—but none of us felt like bothering to investigate them. We saw other tunnels, too, with METRO on them. Beanpole decided they were most likely places where people had got on and off the underground Shmand-Fair, and I imagine he was right.

We slogged on. The day was declining, and we

were all weary. By the time we had our evening meal—a limited one, because food was beginning to run short and there was no way here of getting more—it was plain that we would have to spend the night in the city. I do not think any of us was keen on going into one of the buildings to sleep, but a distant howling changed our minds for us. If there were a pack of wild dogs near, it would be safer to get off the streets. They did not usually attack people unless they were hungry; but we had no means of knowing the state of their stomachs.

We picked a substantial-looking edifice and went up to the first floor, stamping warily on the stairs to see if they were likely to collapse. Nothing happened, except that dust rose, choking us. We found a room with glass still in its windows. The curtains and the upholstery of the furniture were faded and eaten in holes by moths, but it was still comfortable. I found a big earthenware jar, with a heavy lid, and roses painted on it. When I took the lid off it was full of withered rose petals, their perfume a ghost of summers long ago. There was a piano, larger and differently shaped from any I had seen, and a frame on it with a picture, in black and white, of a lady. I wondered if it was she who had lived here. She was very beautiful, though her hair was different from the way women wear their hair today, with wide dark eyes and a gently smiling mouth. In the night I awoke, and there was the scent still in the air, and moonlight from the window fell across the top of the piano, and I almost thought I could glimpse her there, her slender white fingers moving across the keys—that I could hear phantom music.

It was nonsense, of course, and when I fell asleep again I did not dream of her but of being back in the village, in the den with Jack, in the time when I had not learned to worry over Caps and the Tripods, and when I had thought never to travel farther from Wherton than Winchester; and that no more than once a year.

The moonlight was misleading; in the morning, not only were the clouds back, chasing each other in an endless pursuit of monotonous gray, but a dreary deluge of rain was sheeting down out of the sky. Even though we were anxious to get clear of the city, we did not feel like tackling these conditions. All that was left by way of food was a hunk of cheese, a piece of dried beef, and some of the ship's biscuits. We divided the cheese. There was enough for one more modest meal; after that we would have to go hungry.

Henry found a chess set, and he played a couple of games with Beanpole, who won easily. I then challenged him, and was also beaten. Finally I played against Henry. I expected to beat him, because I thought I had done better against Beanpole, but I lost in about twenty moves. I felt fed up, by this and the weather and being still hungry, and refused his offer to play again. I went and stood by one of the windows, and was glad to note that the sky was clearing, the gray turning in patches into a luminous yellow. Within a quarter of an hour, the rain had stopped and we could go on.

The avenues through which we traveled were gloomy at first, the surface puddled with water or, where trees had split it, of sodden earth, the general wetness continually augmented by drips from the branches above. It was like walking through rain in slow motion, and just as dampening; it was not long before we were all thoroughly soaked. Later, brightness filtered down as the cloud lifted, and the birds seemed to make a second wakening and filled the air with their chatter and song. Drops still fell, but more rarely, and in bare patches where the trees had not got a footing, the sun laid strokes of heat across us. Beanpole and Henry talked more, and more cheerfully. My own spirits did not revive as thoroughly. I felt tired, and a bit shivery, and my mind seemed thick and dull. I hoped I was not getting a cold.

We ate the last of the food in a place where the trees were dense in front of us, without any buildings. The reason lay in the slabs of stone, some upright but more leaning or fallen, which stretched away into the darkness of the wood. The words carved on the nearest one were:

CI-GÎT

MARIANNE LOUISE VAUDRICOURT

13 ANS

DÉCÉDÉE FEVRIER 15 1966

The first two words, Beanpole explained, meant "Here Lies," "ans" was years and "décédée" was died. She had died, at my own age, and been buried here at a time when the city was still throbbing with life. One day at the end of winter. So many people. The wood stretched out, laced with the stones of the dead, across an area in which my village could have been set down several times over.

It was late afternoon when we came at last to the southern edge of the city. The transformation was sudden. We pushed for about a hundred yards through a stretch where the trees were thick, the buildings few and completely in ruins, and emerged into a cornfield, waving green spears in the slanting sunlight. It was a relief to be in the open again, and in cultivated land. With that came awareness that we needed to resume habits of caution: there was a horse plowing several fields away, and in the distance two Tripods stalked the horizon.

Clouds came up again as we traveled south. We found a field of early potatoes, but could find no wood dry enough to start a fire to cook them. Henry and Beanpole ate them raw, but I could not. I had little appetite, anyway, and my head was aching. At night we slept in a ruin well away from any other houses. The roof had fallen at one end, but was still supported at the other; it was wavy, and made of a gray material that looked like stone but was much lighter. I spent the night in a series of heavy sleeps, from which I was wakened by nightmarish dreams, and in the morning I felt more tired than I had been the night before. I suppose I must have looked funny, because Henry asked me if I were feeling ill. I snapped something back at him, and he shrugged and turned his attention to other things. Beanpole said nothing, I think because he noticed nothing. He was much less interested in people than in ideas.

It was a weary day for me. I felt worse as the hours went by. I was determined not to show this, though. At the beginning I had not wanted sympathy from the others because I resented the fact that they appeared to be getting on with each other better than I was with either. After I had rebuffed Henry, my resentment was because neither he nor Beanpole took the matter any farther. I am afraid I got some satisfaction out of feeling ill and carrying on without admitting it. It was a childish way to behave.

At any rate, my lack of appetite did not make much impression because we were all on short commons. I was not bothering anyway, but Henry and Beanpole found nothing. We had reached the wide river, flowing southeast, which the map told us we should follow, and Henry spent half an hour at one place trying, without success, to tickle trout up from under the bank. While he did so, I lay gazing stupefied at the cloudy sky, grateful for the rest.

Toward evening, after endless fields of young wheat and rye, we came in sight of an orchard. There were rows of cherry, plum, and apple. The apples would be small and unripe still, but even from a distance we could see golden and purple plums and cherries black or red-and-white against the green of leaves. The trouble was that the farmhouse was right by the orchard and would have a good view of anyone moving among the long straight ranks of trees. Later, of course, with the onset of darkness, it would be different.

Henry and Beanpole disagreed as to what we should do. Henry wanted to stay, where there was an assurance of some kind of food at least, and wait for the chance to get at it; Beanpole was for pressing on, hoping to find something else, or something better, in the couple of hours' light that remained. I got no pleasure, this time, out of their opposition—I was feeling too heavy and ill to bother. I supported Henry, but only because I was desperate for the rest. Beanpole gave in, as always with a good grace, and we settled down to let the time pass.

When they tried to rouse me to go with them, I paid no heed, being too sunk in lethargy and general wretchedness, and eventually they left me and went off on their own. I had no idea how much later it was that they came back, but I was aware of them trying to rouse me again, offering me fruit and also cheese, which Beanpole had managed to steal from the dairy which abutted on the farmhouse. I could not eat anything—could not be bothered to try—and for the first time they appreciated that I was ill, and not merely sulking. They whispered together, and then they half-lifted, half-dragged me to my feet and hauled me away, supporting me between them.

I learned later that there was an old shed at the

far end of the orchard which did not seem to be in use, and they thought it best to get me there: rain was threatening again and it did rain during the night. I was aware only of stumbling and being pulled along, and at last being allowed to collapse on an earth floor. There were more sweating sleeps after that, and more dreams, from one of which I emerged shouting.

The next thing I realized with any precision was that a dog was growling nearby. Shortly afterward, the door of the shed was flung open, and a shaft of hot sunlight fell on my face, and I saw the dark outline of a gaitered man against the light. It was followed by more confusion, by loud voices in a strange tongue. I tried to struggle to my feet, but fell back.

And the next thing after that, I was lying in cool sheets, in a soft bed, and a grave, dark-eyed girl, in a blue, turban-like cap, was bending over me. I looked past her, in wonder, at my surroundings: a high white ceiling, worked in arabesque, walls of dark-paneled wood, hangings of thick crimson velvet around the bed. I had never known such luxury.

SIX

THE CASTLE OF THE RED TOWER

H ENRY AND BEANPOLE HAD REALIZED, THE
morning after my collapse, that I was not well
enough to travel. They could, of course, have
left me and gone on by themselves. Barring that,
they had a choice either of dragging me farther away
from the farmhouse, or of staying in the hut and
hoping not to be observed. As far as the first was
concerned, there was no other shelter in sight and,
although the rain had stopped, the weather was not
promising. And the hut did not look as though it
were used much. Anyway, they decided to stay where
they were. In the early morning they crept out and

got more plums and cherries and returned to the hut to eat them.

The men with the dogs came an hour or two later. They were never sure whether this was by accident, whether they had been seen earlier and their return to the hut marked, or whether Beanpole had left signs of his entry into the dairy and, with the cheese missing, the men were making a routine check of the outbuildings. What mattered was that the men were at the door, and a dog with them—an ugly brute, standing as high as a small donkey, its teeth bared in a snarl. There was nothing they could do but surrender.

Beanpole had previously worked out an emergency plan for a situation such as this, to get over the difficulty that neither I nor Henry spoke his language. We were to be cousins of his and both deaf-mutes— we were to say nothing, and pretend we could hear nothing. This is what happened; simple enough as far as I was concerned since I was unconscious. It had been Beanpole's idea that this would allay suspicion so that, even if they kept us prisoner, they would not put too strong a guard on us, giving us a better chance of escaping when opportunity offered. I do not know if it would have worked—certainly I was in no state to make an escape from anything— but it fell out that things took a very different turn from anything we had envisioned. It just so happened that, on that particular morning, the Comtesse de la Tour Rouge was making a progress through the district and called with her retinue at the farm.

Care of the sick, and the distribution of largesse, were customary with ladies of the nobility and gentry: when Sir Geoffrey's wife, Lady May, was alive, she used to do this around Wherton: one of my earliest memories was of receiving from her a big red apple and a sugar pig, and touching my cap in reply. With the Comtesse, though, as I grew to know, generosity and care of others was not a matter of duty but sprang from her own nature. She was a gentle and kind person in herself and suffering in another creature—human or animal—was a grief to her. The farmer's wife had scalded her legs weeks before and was now quite recovered, but the Comtesse needed to reassure herself of that. At the farm she was told of the three boys who had been caught hiding—two of them deaf-mutes and one of those in a fever. She took charge of us all right away.

It was a sizable company. Nine or ten of her ladies were with her, and three knights had ridden out with them. There were also esquires and grooms. Beanpole and Henry were put up in front of grooms, but I was set on the saddle-bow of one of the knights, with his belt tied around to keep me from slipping off. I remember nothing of the journey, which is perhaps as well. It was more than ten miles back to the castle, a good deal of it over rough country.

The face bending over me when I awoke was that of the Comtesse's daughter, Eloise.

Le Château de la Tour Rouge stands on high ground, overlooking a confluence of two rivers. It is very ancient, but has had old parts rebuilt and others added from time to time. The tower itself is new, I fancy, because it is of a strange red stone quite unlike the stones used elsewhere in the building. In it are the staterooms and the rooms of the family, where I was put to bed.

The tower is freestanding on the side that looks

down to the river and the plain, but other buildings adjoin at the rear and on either side. There are the kitchens, storerooms, servants' quarters, kennels, stables, forge—all the workaday places. And the knights' quarters, which are well-kept and decorated houses though at this time only three unmarried knights were living in them, the rest having their own houses within easy reach of the castle.

Part of the knights' quarters was given up to the esquires. These were boys, the sons of knights mostly, who were being trained to knighthood, and Henry and Beanpole, by the orders of the Comtesse, were put among them. They quickly realized that there was no immediate danger of being taken for Capping, and decided to wait and see what happened.

For me, meanwhile, there was the confusion of sickness and delirium. They told me later that I was in a fever for four days. I was aware of strange faces, particularly of the dark-eyed face beneath the blue turban, which gradually became familiar. My sleep, by degrees, became more restful, the world into which I awakened less incoherent and distorted.

Until I awoke, feeling myself again, though weak, and the Comtesse was sitting beside my bed, with Eloise standing a little farther off.

The Comtesse smiled, and said, "Are you better now?"

A resolution I must keep . . . Of course. I must not talk. I was a deaf-mute. Like Henry. Where was Henry? My eyes searched the room. At the high window, curtains moved in a breeze. I could hear voices from outside, and the clang of iron.

"Will," the Comtesse said, "you have been very ill, but you are better now. You need only to grow strong."

I must not talk . . . And yet—she had called me by my name! And was speaking to me in English.

She smiled again. "We know the secret. Your friends are all right. Henry and Zhan-pole—Beanpole, as you call him."

There was no point in going on pretending. I said, "They told you?"

"In a fever, it is not possible to control one's tongue. You were determined not to talk, and said so, aloud. In the English speech."

I turned my head away, in shame. The Comtesse said, "It does not matter. Will, look at me."

Her voice, soft but strong, compelled me to turn my head, and I saw her properly for the first time. Her face was too long for her ever to have been beautiful, but it had a gentleness that was lovely, and her smile glowed. Her hair curled around her shoulders, deep black but touched with white, the silvery lines of the Cap showing above the high forehead. She had large, gray, honest eyes.

I asked, "Can I see them?"

"Of course you can. Eloise will tell them to come."

They left the three of us alone. I said, "I gave it away. I didn't mean to. I'm sorry."

Henry said, "You couldn't help it. Are you all right now?"

"Not bad. What are they going to do with us?"

"Nothing, as far as I can see." He nodded at Beanpole. "He knows more than I do."

Beanpole said, "They are not like the villagers, or townsmen. The villagers, finding us, might have called the Tripods, but these not. They think it good for boys to leave their homes. Their own sons go far away."

I suppose I was a little confused still. I said, "Then they might help us!"

Beanpole shook his head, sunlight flashing from the lenses in front of his eyes.

"No. After all, they are Capped. They have different customs, but they obey the Tripods. They are still slaves. They treat us kindly, but they must not know our plans."

I said, with a new alarm, "If I talked . . . I might have said something about the White Mountains."

Beanpole shrugged. "If so, they have thought it was a fever dream. They suspect nothing, believing only that we are wanderers, you two from the land beyond the sea. Henry took the map, from your jacket. We have it safe."

I had been thinking hard. I said, "Then you'd better make a break for it, while you can."

"No. It will be weeks before you are fit to travel."

"But you two can get away. I'll follow when I am able. I remember the map well enough."

Henry said to Beanpole, "It might be a good idea."

I felt a pang at that. For me to suggest it was noble self-sacrifice; having the proposal accepted without demur was less pleasant. Beanpole said, "That is not good. If two go, leaving the other, perhaps they will start to wonder. They may come hunting for us. They have horses, and enjoy to hunt. A change from deer or foxes, no?"

"What do you suggest, then?" Henry asked. I could see he was not persuaded. "If we stay, they'll Cap us eventually."

"That is why staying is better for now," Beanpole said. "I have been talking with some of the boys. In a few weeks there is the tournament."

"The tournament?" I asked.

"It is held twice a year," Beanpole said, "in spring and summer. They have feasts, games, contests and jousting between the knights. It lasts five days, and at the end is their Capping Day."

"And if we are still here then . . . ," Henry said.

"We are offered for Capping. True. But we will not be here. You will be strong by then, Will. And during the time of the tournament there is always much confusion. We can get away, and not be missed for a day, perhaps two or three. Also, having more exciting things to do here at the castle, I think they will not trouble to hunt us anyway."

Henry said, "You mean, do nothing till then?"

"This is sensible."

I saw that it was. It also relieved me from the thought, more terrifying the more I contemplated it, of being abandoned. I said, trying to make my voice sound indifferent:

"You two must decide."

Henry said reluctantly, "I suppose it is the best thing."

The boys came up to me from time to time, but I saw more of the Comtesse, and Eloise. Occasionally, the Comte looked in. He was a big, ugly man, who had, I learned, a great reputation for bravery, in tournaments and at the hunt. (Once, unhorsed, he had met a huge wild boar face to face, and killed it with his dagger.) With me he was awkward but amiable, given to poor jokes at which he laughed a lot. He spoke a little English, too, but badly, so that often I could not understand him: mastery of other tongues was regarded as an accomplishment better suited to the ladies.

I had known very little about the nobility before this. At Wherton, the servants from the Manor House kept to themselves, not mixing much with people from the village. Now I saw them at close quarters and, lying in bed, had time to think about them, and particularly about their attitude toward the Tripods. As Beanpole had suggested, it was not, in essence, different from that of humbler people. Take, for, instance, their tolerance of boys running away from home. This would not have been the case with villagers, either here or at Wherton, but that was because their lives were of another pattern: the sea captains at Rumney took to the notion well enough. To the nobility, it was right that ladies should be gracious and accomplished in certain things, and that men should be brave. There were no wars, as there had once been, but there were a number of ways in which courage could be shown. And a boy who ran away from his humdrum life, even though not noble, in their view displayed spirit.

The bitter thing was that all the spirit, all the gallantry, was wasted. For even more than their inferiors, they accepted and looked forward to being Capped. It was a part of becoming a knight, or of turning from girl to lady. Thinking of this, I saw how good things could be meaningless in isolation. What value did courage have, without a free and challenging mind to direct it?

Eloise taught me how to speak their language. It was easier than I expected; we had plenty of time at our disposal, and she was a patient teacher. Pronouncing the words gave me the most difficulty—I had to learn to make sounds in my nose and sometimes despaired of getting them right. Beanpole's name, I learned, was not Zhan-pole, but Jean-Paul, and even those simple syllables took some mastering.

I was allowed up after a few days. My old clothes had disappeared and I was given new ones. These consisted of sandals, undergarments, a pair of shorts and a shirt, but they were of much finer material than I had been used to and were more colorful; the shorts were a creamy color and the shirt, on that first day, was dark red. I found to my surprise that they were taken away each night for laundering and replaced by fresh.

Eloise and I wandered about the rooms and grounds of the castle contentedly. At home, I had not mixed much with girls, and had been ill at ease when I could not avoid their company, but with her I felt no strain nor awkwardness. Her English, like her mother's was very good, but soon she insisted on speaking to me in her own tongue. By this means, I picked up things quickly. She would point to the window, and I would say, *"la fenêtre,"* or beyond, and I would say, *"le ciel."*

I was still supposed not to be well enough to join the other boys. If I had made a fuss, I imagine I might have been permitted to do so, but I accepted the situation willingly. Being docile at the moment would improve our chance of escaping later. And it seemed ungenerous to rebuff Eloise's kindness. She was the only child of the Comte and Comtesse remaining in the castle, her two brothers being esquires at the house of a great Duke in the south, and she did not seem to have friends among the other girls. I gathered she had been lonely.

There was another reason, too. It still rankled that Henry should have displaced me with Beanpole, and when I ran into them I had an impression of a companionship, a complicity, which I did not share. Their life, of course, was quite different from mine. It is even possible they were a little jealous of the cosseting I was getting. What was certain was that we had little to talk about as far as our present existences were concerned and could not, for safety, discuss the more important enterprise which we did have in common.

So I willingly turned from them to Eloise. She had, like her mother, a soothing gentleness. Like her, she had a deep feeling for all living creatures, from the people about her to the hens that scratched in the dust outside the servants' quarters. Her smile was her mother's, but that was the only real physical likeness. For Eloise was pretty, not only when she smiled but in the stillness of repose. She had a small oval face, with an ivory skin that could flush a strange, delicate color, and deep brown eyes.

I wondered about the color of her hair. She always wore the same turban-like cap, covering her head completely. One day I asked her about it. I put the question in my halting French, and either she did not understand me, or affected not to; so I asked her bluntly, in English. She said something then, but in her own language and too fast for me to grasp the meaning.

We were standing in the small triangular garden, formed by the castle's prow where it jutted out toward the river. There was no one else in sight, no sound except from the birds and some of the esquires shouting as they rode across the tilt-yard behind us. I was irritated by her evasiveness, and I made a grab, half-playful, half-annoyed, at the turban. It came away at my touch. And Eloise stood before me, her head covered by a short dark fuzz of hair, and by the silver mesh of the Cap.

It was a possibility that had not occurred to me. Being fairly small of stature, I had the habit of assuming that anyone older than myself must be taller, and she was an inch or two shorter than I. Her features, too, were small and delicate. I stared at her, dumbfounded, blushing, as she was, but fiery red rather than the faint flush of rose.

I realized from her reaction that I had done something outrageous, but I did not know how outrageous. For girls, as I have said, Capping was a part of the process of becoming a lady. When she had recovered herself, and wound the turban back on, Eloise explained something of this, speaking in English so that I would be sure to understand her fully. Here girls wore turbans for the ceremony, and were returned by the Tripods still wearing them. For six months after that, no one, not even the Comtesse, was supposed to see her naked head. At the end of that time, a special ball would be held, and there, for the first time since the Capping, she would show herself. And I had torn the turban from her, as I would have pulled off a boy's cap, fooling about in school!

She spoke not in anger or reproach, but patiently. She felt a great shame that I had seen her head, but her real concern was for what might have happened to me if the incident had been seen by others. A severe flogging would have been the first, but probably not the last of my punishments. It was said that a man had been killed once for such an offense.

My feelings, as I listened, were mixed. There was some gratitude for her wanting to protect me: but resentment, too, at being judged, even gently, by a code of conduct which meant nothing to me. At Wherton the girls, like the boys, had come back bare-headed from Capping. My feelings about Eloise herself were also jumbled and uncertain. I had traveled a long road since leaving the village, not only in hard reality but in my attitude toward people. More and more I had come to see the Capped as lacking what seemed to me the essence of humanity, the vital spark of defiance against the rulers of the world. And I had despised them for it—despised even, for all their kindness to me and their goodness, the Comte and Comtesse.

But not Eloise. I had thought her free, like myself. I might even have come to the idea—its beginnings, I think, were in my mind already—that when we set off once more for the White Mountains, there might not be three of us, but four. All this was rendered futile by the sight of her bare head. I had come to think of her as my friend: perhaps more. But now I knew that she belonged, irretrievably, body and soul, to the Enemy.

The episode disturbed us both a great deal. For Eloise there had been two blows—to her modesty, and to her idea of me. My snatching at her turban had shocked her. Even though she knew it was done in ignorance, it was the mark, in her eyes, of a barbarian; and a barbarian in one thing is likely to be barbarous in others. She was uncertain of me.

With me, what had emerged was not uncertainty, but the reverse. Nothing could come of my friendship with her: a hard black line had been scored across it. The only thing to do was forget about it and concentrate on the important thing, which was getting to the White Mountains. I saw Henry and Beanpole later that day, and suggested we should make a break at once: I was sure I was strong enough to travel. But Beanpole was insistent on waiting for the tournament, and this time Henry backed him up wholeheartedly. I was angry, and disappointed—I had expected him to support me. It was the alliance again, and again I was excluded. I left them abruptly.

On the stairs, I met the Comte, who grinned at me, slapped me heavily on the back, and said that I looked better but still needed fattening. I must eat plenty of venison. There was nothing like venison for building up the skinny ones. I went on up to the parlor and found Eloise there, her face golden in the lamplight. She smiled at me in welcome. Uncertainty could not affect her constancy and loyalty; they were so deeply ingrained in her nature.

So we continued our companionship, though there was a new wariness between us. Now that I was stronger, we could range farther afield. Horses were saddled for us, and we rode out of the castle gates and down the hill into meadows thick with summer flowers. I knew how to ride, after a fashion, and I soon became proficient, as I was rapidly becoming proficient in the language of this country.

There were some days of cloud and rain, but more of sunshine, in which we rode through warm scented land, or, dismounting, sat and watched the river where the trout leapt, silver out of silver. We visited houses of the knights, and were given fruit drinks and little creamy cakes by their ladies. In the evenings we would sit in the Comtesse's parlor, talking to her or listening to her while she sang, to the accompaniment of a round long-necked instrument whose strings she plucked. Often, while we were there, the Comte would come in, and stay with us, for once quiet.

The Comte and Comtesse made it plain that they liked me. I think it was partly because of their sons having gone away. This was the custom, and it would not have occurred to them to challenge it, but they grieved for their absence. There were other boys in the castle of noble stock, but they lived in the knights' quarters, only joining the family for supper, which was served in the hall at a table where thirty or forty dined at once. I, through being ill and brought into the tower, had become a part of the family as they had never been.

But although I knew they were fond of me, a conversation I had with the Comtesse one day startled me. We were alone together, since Eloise was having a dress fitted. She was embroidering a piece of cloth, and I was watching in fascination the way her fingers moved, deftly and swiftly, making the tiny stitches. She talked as she worked, her voice low and warm, with a slight huskiness that Eloise also had. She asked about my health—I told her I was very well—and if I were happy at the castle. I assured her that I was. Then she said:

"I am glad of that. Perhaps if you are happy, you will not want to leave us."

It had been taken for granted that the three of us would be presented at the Capping Day following the tournament. The assumption had been that after that, the restlessness of our boyhood having departed, we would return to our homes to take up the life that was expected of us as adults. It puzzled me to hear the Comtesse speak of not wanting to leave.

She went on, "Your friends, I think, would wish to go. Room could be found for them, as servants, but I feel they would be happier in their own villages. For you, though, it is different."

I looked from her hands to her face.

"How, my Lady?"

"You are not noble, but nobility can be granted. It lies in the gift of the King, and the King is my cousin." She smiled. "You did not know that? He owes me a debt for a whipping I saved him when he was an un-Capped boy, like you. There will be no difficulty about this, Guillaume."

Guillaume was their way of saying my name. She had told me that, but she had never used it to address me before. My head was spinning a little. Even though I had grown used to the castle and the life that was lived here, it still did not seem entirely real to me. And this talk of kings . . . There was a king in England, too, who lived somewhere in the north. I had never seen him, nor ever expected to.

She was telling me that I could stay—that she wanted me to stay—not as a servant but as a knight. I could have servants of my own, and horses, and armor made for me so that I could ride in the tournaments, and a place in the family of the Comte de la Tour Rouge. I looked at her, and knew that she was quite in earnest. I did not know what to say.

The Comtesse smiled, and said, "We can talk of this again, Guillaume. There is no hurry."

It is not easy to write about what followed.

My first reaction to what the Comtesse had said

was of being flattered, but not impressed. Was I to abandon my hope of freedom, surrender the mastery of my mind, for the sake of wearing jeweled leather and having other men touch their caps to me? The notion was absurd. Whatever privileges I was given, I would still be a sheep among sheep. In the morning, though, waking early, I thought of it again. I rejected it again, too, firmly but less quickly, and with a feeling of being virtuous in doing so. To accept would be to let down the others—Henry and Beanpole, the Vagrant Ozymandias, Captain Curtis, all the free men in the White Mountains. I would not do that: nothing would tempt me to it.

The insidious thing was that temptation should have entered into it at all. From the moment the idea ceased to be unthinkable, I could not let it alone. Of course, I was not going to do it, but if . . . My mind ran on the possibilities, despite myself. I had already learned enough of the language to be able to talk, though in an accent they smiled at, with others in the castle. There was, it seemed, so much to look forward to. After the tournament there would be the Harvest Feast, and then the hunting. They spoke of riding out on sharp autumn mornings, with frost making the grass crackle around the horses' legs, of the hounds baying along the hillside, the chase and the kill, and jogging home to blazing fires and meat carved from the spit turning in the great hearth of the dining hall. And later, the Christmas Feast, lasting twelve days, when the jugglers and singers and strolling players came. Then the spring, and hawking: loosing the falcon to wheel up into the empty blue and plunge down out of it like a bolt on her prey. And so summer, and the tournaments again, filling out the year.

During this time, too, my attitude to the people around me was changing. In Wherton, the division between boy and man was drawn more sharply than here. All adults there, even my parents, had been strangers. I had respected them, admired or feared them, even loved them, but I had not known them as I was coming to know those at the castle. And the better I knew them, the harder it was to make a sweeping condemnation. They were Capped, they accepted the Tripods and all they stood for, but that did not prevent them from being, as I had seen in the

Comte and Comtesse and Eloise and now in others, warmhearted, generous and brave. And happy.

For that, it increasingly seemed to me, was the crux of it. Before Capping there might be doubts and uncertainties and revulsion; perhaps these people had known them, too. When the Cap was put on, the doubts vanished. How great a loss was that? Was it a loss at all? The Tripods, apart from the act of Capping itself, did not seem to interfere much with men. There had been the incident at sea, when they had threatened to swamp the *Orion*. Ships had been sunk by them, Captain Curtis had said—but how many more had been sunk by tempests, or through striking rocks? Ozymandias had spoken of men working in mines underground to get metals for the Tripods, of the Tripods hunting men, of human beings serving them in their cities. But even if those things were true, they must happen far away. None of it touched this secure and pleasant life.

Again and again I returned to the most important consideration: loyalty to Henry and Beanpole and the others. But even that, as the days went by, proved less convincing. In an attempt to reassure myself, I began to seek the other two out. I broached again the idea of our escaping at once, but they turned it down flatly. I had the impression that they did not much want to talk to me, and were impatient for me to leave them. I would go away, resenting their coolness but perhaps also a little glad of it. If one is seeking reasons for disloyalty, it is useful to find something one can resent.

And there was Eloise. We walked and rode and talked together, and gradually the wariness and constraint that had come between us after the incident in the garden was overlaid and buried by the daily commerce of our friendship: we were at ease again, contented with each other's company. One day I took a boat, and rowed upriver to an island we had seen, and we picnicked there. It was a hot day, but cool in the long grass under the shade of the trees, and dragonflies and red and yellow butterflies danced in the air above the tumbling water. I had not spoken to her of what the Comtesse had said, but she herself mentioned it. She took it for granted that I would stay, and I felt a strange shock of pleasure at that. A future here, in this rich lovely country, in the castle, with Eloise . . .

Providing the Capping was a success, I reminded myself. But why should it not be? Captain Curtis's warning belonged to the time when this language had been meaningless gibberish to me. Now, even though I was still far from speaking it perfectly, I understood it. Nor was I likely to become a Vagrant through resisting, when there was so much to gain by acquiescence.

I reminded myself of something else—of what I had thought as I lay in bed, recovering from the fever. That nothing mattered, nothing was of value, without a mind that challenged and inquired. The mood seemed far away, unreal. The Tripods had conquered men when they were at the height of their power and magnificence, capable of building the great-cities, ships as big as a village, perhaps vaster wonders still. If our ancestors, with all their strength, had failed, how pitiful was the defiance of a handful of men clinging to the slopes of barren mountains. And if there were no hope of defeating them, what were the true alternatives? To live wretchedly, like a hunted animal, suffering hardship and despair—or this life, with its fullness and security and happiness.

Rowing back, I found the Watch slipping down to my wrist, hampering my efforts. I had thought at first that the Comtesse and others might be curious about it and want to know how a boy had come by such a possession; but they had shown no interest at all in it. They kept no relics of the skill of the ancients, and time meant nothing to them. There was a sundial in the courtyard, and that was enough. Now, resting on my oars, I took the Watch off and, asking her to look after it for me, tossed it to Eloise. But either I threw it badly or she mishandled the catching: it fell over the side. I had one glimpse of it before it vanished in the green depths. Eloise was distressed, and I comforted her, telling her not to worry: it was no loss. Nor, at that moment, was it.

The time of the tournament was fast approaching. There was an air of excitement and bustle. Great tents were set up in the meadows below, for those who could not be housed in the castle itself. From morning till night the air rang with the sound of armorers, the tilt-yard with cries as the mock-jousts went on. I took a hand myself, and found I could hit the ring tolerably well, riding with my knees.

My mind still worried at the subject. The point of loyalty, for instance. Loyalty to whom? The men in the White Mountains did not even know of my existence—to Ozymandias and Captain Curtis I had been just another boy to be sent south, one of dozens. And Henry and Beanpole? Did they want me with them, anyway? They did not give the impression of doing so. Would they not rather be on their own?

The first morning it rained, but the sky cleared for the afternoon and the preliminary jousts took place. I saw Henry and Beanpole afterward, on the trampled field where servants were picking up and clearing away the litter. The castle walls, and the hard finger of the tower, stood out against the setting sun.

Beanpole explained: early next morning was the time to make a break, at dawn, before the kitchen servants were awake. They had put food aside, in their packs. Mine had disappeared, along with my old clothes, but it did not matter, Beanpole said, if I could not find it or anything similar: they had enough for me as well. I was to meet them below the castle gate, at the appointed time.

I shook my head. "I'm not coming."

Beanpole asked, "Why, Will?"

Henry said nothing, but stood with a smile on his broad face, that I felt I hated, at this moment, even more than I had at home in Wherton. His thoughts, and contempt, were plain.

I said, "If you two go there is a chance you will not be missed, things being confused as they are. But I will be. They will notice that I am not at breakfast, and look for me."

Henry said, "True enough, Beanpole. The Comte is bound to miss his adopted son."

I had not realized that that suggestion had leaked out, though I suppose it was inevitable that it should. Beanpole stared at me, his eyes showing nothing behind the lenses.

I said, "I'll give you a day to get clear, two perhaps. I'll follow. I'll try to catch up with you; but don't wait for me."

Henry laughed. "We won't!"

I was telling myself that I had still not come to a decision. It was true that it would be easier for the others to get clear without me, and true that I could follow on after—I knew the map by heart. But true also that tomorrow, on the second day, the Queen of the Tournament was chosen by the assembled knights. And I was sure the choice would fall on Eloise, not because she was the Comte's only daughter, but because, without doubt, she was the most beautiful that would be there.

Beanpole said slowly, "Very well. Perhaps it is best."

I said, "Good luck."

"And you." His head shook slightly. "Good luck, Will."

I turned, and walked up the hill to the castle. I heard Henry say something I did not catch, but I did not look back.

SEVEN

THE TRIPOD

I AWOKE IN THE EARLY DAWN, AND REALIZED there was still time to slip away and join the others, but I did not move from my bed. The window of my room looked south, and I could see that the sky was a deep dark blue—one bright star stood out. I was glad that they would have good weather for traveling, but glad also that it looked as though it would be fine for the second day of the tournament, and the choosing of the Queen. I lay and stared at the sky until I drifted back into sleep, to be awakened a second time by the servant girl tapping on my door. The blue of sky was pale now, and brushed with gold.

There was no mention of Beanpole and Henry—no one seemed to have missed them. It was not surprising that this should be so: today the tournament was in full swing, everyone was cheerful and excited, and after breakfast we made our way down to the field and the pavilions. But not Eloise. She would come down later with the other ladies who offered themselves for the knights' choosing. We took our places in the pavilion, and while we waited a singer entertained us with ballads. Then came the hush, as the ladies entered the ring.

There were eleven of them, and ten were dressed in great finery, with dresses that had much silver and gold thread and needed to be held up behind by serving girls so that they would not trail in the dust. Their heads were bare, their hair piled high and secured with combs that flashed and dazzled in the sunlight. The eleventh was Eloise. She wore, of course, the turban on her head, and her dress was simple—dark blue, trimmed with delicate white lace. As youngest she came last, with no servant accompanying her. To a low beat of drums, the ladies walked across the field to where the knights stood assembled in front of the Comte's pavilion, and, as the fanfare of trumpets sounded, remained there, their heads cast down.

One by one, they stepped forward. It was the custom that, as each did so, the knight who chose her unsheathed his sword, and raised it. After the first two or three, there was no doubt what the result would be. Out of the thirty or forty knights, a couple saluted each lady, so that none should be shamed. This happened with all the gorgeously appareled ten. And so Eloise stepped forward, in her simple dress, and the swords swept up like a forest of silver in the sun, and first the knights and then those watching shouted their acclamation, and I wanted to cry and laugh at the same time.

She came forward, the other ladies following, and stood there, grave and brave in her dignity, while her father, the Comte, carefully fitted the crown over the turban on her head. And her subjects filed past to kiss her hand, myself among them.

I did not see her to speak to for the rest of that day, but I did not mind this. She had her duty, to preside, to give prizes to the victors, and for me there was excitement enough in the tournament itself, in cheering on those I had come to know, and in the whole atmosphere of feasting and merrymaking.

There was only one chilling moment. As the second session of the day began, there was a strange sound far away, which became louder. It was a constant repetition on five notes, a metallic clanging, and although I had not heard this particular call, I knew it could only be a Tripod. I looked in the direction from which it was coming, but the castle stood in the way and I could see nothing. I looked also at the people around me, and saw that none showed more than a mild interest: the contest going on in the ring, with four knights on each side, continued to hold their attention. Even when the hemisphere rocked around the outline of the castle, and the Tripod came and stood towering over the field, its feet planted in the river, there was no sign of the fear and uneasiness which shivered along my spine.

It was plain that this was not an unusual event, that a Tripod always attended the tournament and that they found no cause for alarm in it. Of course, they were more accustomed to the sight of the Tripods than we had been at Wherton, where we only saw one on Capping Day. Almost every day one saw them here, singly or in groups, striding across the valley. I had grown used to the sight, too—at that distance. Being right under its shadow was different. I looked up at it, fearfully. I noticed that, around the sides of the hemisphere and in the base, were circles of what looked like green-tinted glass. Did it see through those? I supposed so. I had not noticed them before, because at Wherton I had never dared look at a Tripod closely. Nor did I for long now. One of the circles had me directly in its view. I dropped my eyes to watch the tournament, but my mind was not on it.

And yet, as time passed, my disquiet subsided. The Tripod had made no sound since it took up its position by the castle, and it did not move at all. It was just there, presiding or watching or merely standing up against the sky, and one became inured to its presence, and regardless of it. After an hour, I was cheering on a favorite of mine, the Chevalier de Trouillon, with no thought beyond the hope that, after two falls on each side, he would win the final tilt. He did, and his opponent rolled in the beaten and withered grass, and like everyone else I cheered him to the echo.

There was a feast that evening, as there would be every night of the tournament, and since the weather was fine, it was held in the courtyard. The household of the Comte, and those knights who had their ladies with them, were seated, and food was brought to them; the rest served themselves from the tables at the side, which were laden with different kinds of fish and meat, vegetables and fruit and sweets and puddings, and where tall jugs of wine stood. (Not a great deal was drunk while we were there, but the knights stayed on after the ladies had gone in to the tower, and torches were lit, and there was singing, and some shouting, until very late.) I could not count the number of dishes. It was not merely the different kinds of meat and fowl and fish, but the different ways each kind might be prepared and sauced. They counted eating a fine art in a way that I do not think even Sir Geoffrey would have understood, and certainly no one in Wherton itself.

I went in with the ladies, very full and happy. The Tripod was still where it had been all afternoon, but one saw it only as a dark shape against the stars, something remote and almost unimportant. From the window of my room, I could not see it at all. There was the bright shawl of the Milky Way, and the torches down in the courtyard—nothing else. I heard a tap on my door, and called *"Entrez!"* I turned to see it open, and Eloise slipped in.

She was still wearing the blue gown trimmed with lace, though she had put the crown aside. Before I could speak, she said, "Will, I cannot stay. I managed to get away, but they will be looking for me."

I understood that. As Queen of the Tournament, her position was special. While it lasted, there could be no pleasant talks, no wandering away. I said, "They chose well. I am glad, Eloise."

She said, "I wanted to say good-bye, Will."

"It will not be for long. A few days. Then, when I am Capped . . ."

She shook her head. "I shall not see you again. Did you not know?"

"But I am to stay here. Your father said so, only this morning."

"You will stay, but not I. Did no one tell you?"

"Tell me what?"

"When the tournament is over, the Queen goes to serve the Tripods. It is always done."

I said stupidly, "Serve them where?"

"In their city."

"But for how long?"

"I have told you. Forever."

Her words shocked me, but the look on her face was more shocking still. It was a kind of rapt devotion, the expression of someone who hugs in secret her heart's desire.

Dazed, I asked her, "Your parents know this?"

"Of course."

They had, as I knew, deeply missed their sons, sent away for a few years only to learn knighthood in another household. And this was their daughter, whom they loved perhaps more dearly still, and she was to go to the Tripods and never return . . . and all day long I had seen them happy and rejoicing. It was monstrous. I burst out: "You must not! I won't let it happen." She smiled at me, and gave a small shake of the head, like an adult listening to a child's wild talk. "Come away with me," I said. "We'll go where there are no Tripods. Come away now!"

She said, "When you are Capped, you will understand."

"I will not be Capped!"

"You will understand." She drew a gasp of breath. "I am so happy." She came forward, took my hands and, leaning forward, kissed me, a peck of a kiss on the cheek. "So happy!" she repeated. She went back to the door, while I stood there. "I must go now. Good-bye, Will. Remember me. I will remember you."

And was gone, out of the door, her feet pattering away down the corridor, before I could come out of my trance. I went to the door then, but the corridor was empty. I called, but there was only my voice echoing back to me from stone walls: I even took a few steps to follow her, before I stopped. It was no good. Not only because there would be other people there, but because of Eloise herself. "I will remember you." She had forgotten me already, in any sense that truly mattered. All her mind was concentrated on the Tripods. Her masters had called, and she was going to them gladly.

I went back into my room, and undressed, and tried to sleep. There were too many kinds of horror. Horror at what had happened to Eloise. Horror of the creatures who could do this sort of thing to others. Horror, above all, at how closely I had come to falling—no, to throwing myself—into something beside which suicide was clean and good. What had happened was not Eloise's fault. She had accepted Capping as the countless others had done, not understanding and knowing no alternative. But I had understood, and had known better. I thought of the blankness in Beanpole's face, the contempt in Henry's, the last time I had seen them, and was ashamed.

The noise of revelry in the courtyard had long died away. I lay, tossing and turning, and saw a softer wider light than starlight coloring the frame of the window. I halted my thoughts in their futile round of self-accusation; and began to make plans.

• • •

It was dark inside the house as I went quietly down the stairs, but outside it was light enough to see my way. There was no one about, nor would be for a couple of hours, at least. Even the servants slept later during the days of tournament. I made my way to the kitchens, and found one of them snoring under a table; presumably he had been too drunk to go to his bed. There was little danger of him waking up. I had brought a pillowslip from my bed, and I piled remnants from the previous night's feast into it: a couple of roast chickens, half a turkey, loaves of bread, cheese and cold sausage. Then I went to the stables.

There was more danger here. The grooms slept on the other side of the horses' stalls, and while they, too, would have drunk their fill, a disturbance among the horses was likely to wake them. The horse I wanted was the one I had been accustomed to riding with Eloise, a chestnut gelding, only about fourteen hands high, called Aristide. He was a somewhat nervous beast, but he and I had grown to know each other, and I relied on that. He stood still, only snorting a couple of times, while I freed him, and came with me like a lamb. Fortunately, there was straw on the floor, muffling his hooves. I lifted his saddle from its place by the door, and then we were clear.

I led him down and out of the gate of the castle before saddling him. He whinnied, but I judged we were far enough away for it not to matter. I tucked the top of the pillowslip under his girth before tightening it, and prepared to mount. Before I did so, I looked about me. Behind lay the castle, dark and sleeping; before me the tournament field, the flaps of the pavilions moving a little in a breeze of morning. On my left . . . I had forgotten about the Tripod, or perhaps assumed that it would have moved away during the night. But it was there, as far as I could see in exactly the same spot. Dark like the castle; and, like the castle, sleeping? It looked as if it were, but I felt a tremor of unease. Instead of mounting and riding down the broad and easy slope, I led him away along the steeper and more difficult path which wound down the side of the rock on which the castle was built, and came out between the meadows and the river. There a line of trees partly shielded it from the view either of the castle or the metal giant standing sentinel among the rushing waters of the river's other branch. Nothing had happened. There was no sound but a water bird that croaked nearby. I mounted Aristide at last, pressed my heels into his flanks, and we were off.

It was true that, as I had said to Henry and Beanpole, although they might get away and their absence not be noticed for a day or two, I would be missed much sooner. Even with the tournament in progress, it was likely that a search party would come after me. Because of this, I had taken the horse. It meant I could put as great a distance as possible between me and any pursuit. If they did not find me within twenty miles of the castle, I felt that I was safe.

The horse also gave me a chance of catching up with Henry and Beanpole. I knew roughly the route they must take; they had a day's start on me, but they were on foot. I was less likely now to be troubled by their being better friends with each other than either was with me. I was very conscious, in the gray light of dawn, of being on my own.

The path led by the riverside for nearly a mile to the ford, where I must cross to the other bank. I had covered about half of this when I heard the sound. The dull clump of a great weight striking the earth, and another, and another. Automatically, even as I glanced back, I was urging Aristide into a gallop. The sight was plain, and horrible. The Tripod had uprooted itself from its post by the castle. It was traveling, steadily and relentlessly, in my wake.

I remember almost nothing about the next few minutes; partly because I was in such an extremity of fear that I could not think straight, and partly, perhaps, because of what happened after. The only thing that comes back clearly is the most terrifying of all—the moment when I felt a band of metal, cold but incredibly flexible, curl around my waist and lift me from Aristide's back. There was a confused impression of rising through the air, feebly struggling, afraid both of what was to happen and, if I did free myself, of falling to the ground already dizzily far below me, looking up at the burnished carapace, seeing the blackness of the open hole which would swallow me, knowing fear as I have never known it before, and screaming, screaming . . . And then blackness.

The sun pressed against my eyelids, warming, turning darkness to a swimming pink. I opened my eyes, and had to shade them at once from its glare. I was lying on my back, on the grass, and the sun, I saw, was standing well above the horizon. That would make it about six o'clock. And it had not been four when . . .

The Tripod.

The jolt of fear shook me, as I remembered. I did not want to search the sky, but knew I must. I saw blue emptiness, fringed by the waving green of trees. Nothing else. I scrambled to my feet, and stared into the distance. There was the castle, and beside it, where it had stood yesterday, where I had seen it as I led Aristide out of the gate, the Tripod. It was motionless, seeming, like the castle itself, rooted in rock.

Fifty yards from me, Aristide cropped the dewy grass, with the contentment of a horse enjoying good pasture. I walked toward him, trying to turn the jumble of my thoughts into some kind of sense. Had it been imaginary, a nightmare, dreamed as a result of a fall from the horse? But the memory of being plucked up through the air came back, sending a shudder through me. I could not doubt that recollection: it had happened—the fear and despair had been real.

Then what? The Tripod had picked me up. Could it be . . . ? I put my hand up to my head and felt hair, and the hardness of my skull, with no mesh of metal. I had not been Capped. With my relief at that came a quick wave of nausea that made me pause and draw breath. I was only a few yards from Aristide and he looked up with a whinny of recognition.

First things first. The castle would be stirring, or at least the servants would. It would be an hour or more before I was missed from my room, but there was no time to waste in getting away—I was still within sight from the ramparts. I took the horse's rein, twisted the stirrup, and swung up into the saddle. Not far ahead the river boiled across the shallows of the ford. I urged him forward, and he responded willingly. Crossing the ford, I looked back again. Nothing had changed, the Tripod had not moved. This time relief was not disabling, but enlivening. Water splashed against Aristide's fetlocks. The breeze was stronger than it had been, carrying a scent that tantalized me before I remembered it. A bush with that scent had grown on the island in the river, where Eloise and I had picnicked, where we had been happy and at ease and she had talked of the future. I reached the far side of the river. A track led through fields of rye, flat and straight for a long way. I pressed Aristide into a canter.

I rode for several hours before I thought it safe to stop. The land was empty at the beginning, but later I passed men making for the fields, or already working there. The first I came on suddenly, cantering around a bend marked by a small copse, and I was confused and apprehensive. But they saluted me as I rode past, and I realized they were saluting the saddle, and the fine clothes I wore: to them I was one of the gentry, a boy taking a ride before breakfast. All the same, I avoided meeting people as far as I could, and was glad when I came out of cultivated land into rough rolling uplands, where I saw nothing but sheep.

There had been time to think about the Tripod—about the amazing fact that I had been caught, and then set free, unharmed, un-Capped, but I came no nearer to a solution. I had to abandon it as one of the incalculabilities that happened with them—a whim, perhaps like the whim that had caused those others to spin around the *Orion*, howling in rage or glee or some other quite different and unfathomable emotion, and then rocket off across the water, away and out of sight. These creatures were nonhuman, and one should not try to give them human motives. All that really mattered was that I *was* free, that my mind was still my own and master, as far as circumstances allowed, of my destiny.

I ate, and drank water from a stream, and mounted and rode again. I thought of those I had left behind at the castle, of the Comte and Comtesse, the knights and esquires I had come to know, of Eloise. I was fairly confident they would not find me now—Aristide's hooves would leave no trace on the short grass and sun-baked earth, and they could not spare long from the tournament for a pursuit. They seemed very far away, not just in terms of distance but as people. I remembered their kindness—the graciousness and sympathy of the Comtesse, the Comte's laughter and his heavy hand on my shoulder—but there was something not quite real about the memories. Except of Eloise. I saw her clearly, and heard her voice, as I had seen and heard her so many times during the past weeks. But the last image was the one that came most sharply and cruelly to mind: the look on her face when she told me she was going to serve the Tripods, and said, "I am so happy—so happy." I kicked Aristide, and he gave a snort of protest, but moved into a gallop across the green sunlit hillside.

The hills rose higher and higher ahead. There was a pass marked on the map, and if I had traveled right by the sun, I should soon be in sight of it. I drew rein on the crest of a ridge and looked down the slope beyond. I thought I saw a gap at about the right place in the line of green and brown, but every-thing trembled in a haze of heat, making identification difficult. But there was something nearer which drew me.

Perhaps half a mile ahead, something moved. A figure—two, toiling up from the fold of ground. I could not identify them yet, but who else could it be, in this deserted spot? I set Aristide to the gallop again.

They turned before I got close, alarmed by the sound of hooves, but long before that I had made sure of them. I came to a halt beside them, and leapt off the horse's back, even now, I am afraid, proud of the horsemanship I had acquired.

Henry stared at me, puzzled, and at a loss for words. Beanpole said, "So you have come, Will."

"Of course," I said. "Why, didn't you think I would?"

EIGHT

FLIGHT AND A FOLLOWER

I TOLD THEM NOTHING OF ELOISE, AND WHAT
had changed my mind. This was not just because
I was ashamed to admit that I had seriously
thought of staying behind, of allowing myself to be
Capped for the sake of the rewards that would follow; though I was bitterly ashamed. It was also
because I did not want to talk about Eloise to anyone. Subsequently, Henry made one or two sly
remarks which obviously referred to her, but I
ignored him. At this time, though, he was still too
shaken by my appearance to say much.

It sounded sensible and well-planned, the way I

told it—that I had thought it best to give them twenty-four hours' start, and then steal a horse and follow them: this gave us all the greatest chance of getting away. I did tell them of my experience with the Tripod. I thought they might be able to cast some light on it, that Beanpole, at least, would be able to work out a theory to account for it, but they were as much at a loss as I was. Beanpole was anxious that I should try to remember if I had actually been taken inside the Tripod, and what it had been like, but of course I could not.

It was Beanpole who said that Aristide must go. I had not thought about this, except in a hazy way of imagining that, if I found the other two again, I could generously let them have turns in riding him, myself remaining his proprietor. But it was true, as Beanpole pointed out, that three boys and a horse, unlike three boys on foot or a single boy on a horse, presented a picture that posed questions in the mind of any who saw them.

Reluctantly, I accepted the fact that I could not keep him. We took off his saddle, because it had the arms of the Tour Rouge stamped on it, and hid it behind a ridge of rock, kicking dirt and piling stones over it to conceal it to some extent. It would be found eventually, but not as soon as Aristide was likely to be. He was a fine horse, and whoever came across him, running free and without harness, might not search too far for an owner. I freed him from his bridle, and he tossed his head, at liberty. Then I gave him a sharp slap on the haunch. He reared, went a few yards, and halted, looking back at me. I thought he was unwilling to leave me, and tried to think of some excuse for keeping him a while longer, but he whinnied, tossed his head again, and trotted away to the north. I turned my head, not wanting to see him go.

So we set off, once more on our way, the three of us once more together. I was very glad of their company, and held my tongue even when Henry, by now recovered, made a few slighting remarks about how hard this must be after the life of luxury which I had enjoyed at the castle. In fact, Beanpole intervened, stopping him. Beanpole, it seemed to me, was taking it for granted that, insofar as there was a leader in our little group, it was he. I did not feel like challenging that, either, at least not at the moment.

I did find the walking tiring—the muscles one used were quite different from those used in riding, and there was no doubt that I was out of condition, as a result of my illness and the protracted indolent convalescence that had followed it. I gritted my teeth, though, and kept up with the others, trying not to show fatigue. But I was glad when Beanpole called a halt for a meal and rest.

That night, too, when we slept out under the stars, with the hard earth under me instead of the down-filled mattress to which I had grown accustomed, I could not help feeling a little sorry for myself. But I was so tired, having had no sleep the night before, that I did not stay long awake. In the morning, though, every individual limb felt sore, as though someone had been kicking me all night long. The day was bright again, and still, without the breeze that had cooled us yesterday. This would be the fourth, the next to last day of the tournament. There would be the mêlée, and riding at the ring. Eloise would still be wearing her crown, awarding prizes to the victors. And after tomorrow . . .

We reached the pass marked on the map, not

long after we set off. We followed a river which came down out of the hills, its course interrupted at times by splashing falls, some of them quite large. Higher up, the map showed a place where another river came close to this one, for a while running almost alongside it, and we came to it before evening.

This second river, except in a few places where it had broken its banks, was oddly straight-sided, and uniform in width. Moreover, it ran on different levels, the divisions between them marked by devices plainly made by the ancients, with rotting timbers and rusting iron wheels and such. Beanpole, of course, worked it all out to his satisfaction. Men had made the second river, digging out its bed and perhaps feeding water into it from the main river. He showed us that, beneath the grass and other vegetation covering the banks, there were bricks, carefully laid and mortared. As for the devices, these were a means of permitting boats to pass from one level of the river to another—a method of filling and draining the short stretch between the two sections that were at different heights. The way he explained it made it sound reasonable, but he was good at making fantastic things seem plausible.

He grew quite enthusiastic about the idea as we traveled alongside the river. This could be—had been, he was sure—an aquatic Shmand-Fair, with boats pulling carriages along the level waters, and people getting on and off at the places where the wheels and things were.

"With your steam-kettle pushing them?" Henry said.

"Why not!"

"Plenty of water for it, anyway."

I said, "Some of the stops seem to have been very close together, and others miles apart. And there are no signs of villages having been there. Only the ruins of a cottage, sometimes not even that."

He said impatiently, "One cannot understand all the things the ancients did. But they built this river, it is certain, and must therefore have used it. It could be fixed to work again."

Where the straight river turned sharply back on itself, toward the north, we left it. The country that followed was much rougher, with even fewer signs of cultivation or human habitation. Food was beginning to be a problem again. We had got through that which we had brought from the castle, and the pickings here were small. At our hungriest, we came on a wild chicken's nest. She had been sitting on a clutch of fourteen eggs, and ten of them we found we could manage to eat, with the aid of the sharp spice of hunger: the rest were bad. We would have eaten her as willingly, if we had been able to catch her.

At last we looked down from the hills into a broad green valley, through which a great river flowed. Far in the distance, other hills rose. Beyond them again, according to the map, were the mountains which marked our journey's end. We had come a long way, and still had far to go. But the valley was patchworked with fields, and one saw houses and farms and villages. There was food down there.

Foraging, though, proved less easy than we had expected. Our first three attempts at raiding were frustrated, twice by furiously barking dogs, the third time by the farmer himself, who woke and came after us, shouting, as we scattered through his yard. We found potato fields, and managed to stave off the worst of our hunger, but raw potato was a poor diet for traveling and living rough on. I thought unhappily of all the food that went to waste at the castle—this, I calculated, would have been Capping Day, when the feasting was on an even more magnificent scale than during the tournament. But, thinking of that, I thought of Eloise, who would not be at this feast. There were worse things than hunger, worse ills than physical discomfort.

The next morning, our luck changed. We had come more than halfway across the valley (having swum the river and afterward let the sun dry us as we lay exhausted on its banks), and were moving into higher country again. There was a village, to which we gave a wide berth, but even from a distance we could see activity down there—flags and banners were out for some local celebration. I thought of Capping, but Beanpole said it was more likely to be one of the many Church feasts they had during the year—these were more common in his land than in England.

We watched for a time, and while we were doing so witnessed an exodus from a farmhouse, a few hundred yards from the copse where we lay. Two traps were brought around to the front door, the horses decorated with ribbons, and people piled into them, dressed in their Sunday clothes. They looked prosperous and well-fed. I said hungrily: "Do you think they've all gone?"

We waited until the traps were out of sight before we made our reconnaissance. Beanpole approached the house, while Henry and I waited nearby. If there were someone in, he would make an excuse and get away. If not . . .

There was not even a dog—perhaps they had taken it with them to the celebration—and we did not have to break in. A window had been left far enough open for me to wriggle through and slip the door bolts for the others. We wasted no time, but headed for the larder. We polished off a half-carved goose and some cold roast pork, and spread brawn on crusty bread. When we had eaten as much as we could, we filled our packs and went, replete and somewhat sluggishly, on our way.

And guiltily? It was the biggest act of piracy, or theft if you like, which we had committed so far.

The bells still rang out in the valley, and a procession was moving along the main street of the village: children in white, followed by their elders. Presumably including the farmer and his wife, who would come back to find their larder stripped. I could imagine my mother's distress, my father's angry contempt, at such pilfering. In Wherton, no stranger was sent away hungry, but the rules of mine and thine were sacrosanct.

The difference was that we were not strangers—we were outlaws. In our pitifully puny way, we were at war. Essentially with the Tripods, but indirectly with all those who, for whatever reason, supported them. Including—I forced myself to stare it in the face—those I had known and been fond of at the Château de la Tour Rouge. Every man's hand was against us in the enemy country through which we marched. We must live by our wits and resources: none of the old rules applied.

Later, we saw a Tripod, coming along the valley, the first we had seen for some days. I thought Beanpole had been wrong, that it was heading for the village and a Capping, but instead of going there it stopped, well clear of habitation, a mile or so from us. It stayed there, as motionless and seemingly inanimate as the one at the castle had been. We went on a little faster than before, and kept in cover as much as we could. Though there seemed little point in it: there was no reason to assume that it was concerned with us, or could even see us. It gave no indication of wanting to follow us. In an hour or so, we lost sight of it.

We saw the Tripod, or a similar one, the next morning, and once again it halted some way from us and stayed there. Again we moved on, and lost it. There was more cloud in the sky than there had been, and there was a blustery wind. We had finished the food we had taken from the farmhouse—Beanpole had wanted to ration it out, but for once Henry and I had overridden him—and did not find any more as the day wore on. We were hungry again, probably the more so because we had eaten well the day before.

Toward evening, we climbed up through fields closely set with plants, supported by sticks, on which were clusters of small green fruit. These would be picked when they were fully grown and ripe, and their juice squeezed out of them to make wine. There had been a few fields of them in the neighborhood of the castle, but I was amazed by how many of them there were here, and how the fields—or terraces, rather—were laid out to catch the rain and sun. I was hungry enough to try one or two of the larger fruits, but they were hard and sour, and I had to spit them out.

We had been sleeping in the open, but we realized that, with the possibility of the weather breaking, it might be a good idea to find some shelter for the night. In fact, we discovered a hut, a rough-and-ready affair set at the junction of three of the fields. Remembering our last experience we were wary of going in, but Beanpole assured us that it was a place that would only be used at the time of picking the fruit, and certainly there was no dwelling in sight—only the long ranks of sticks and plants stretching away in the dusk. It was very bare, with not even a chair or table, but the roof, although it showed the sky in places, would keep most of the rain off us.

It was a relief to have found refuge and shelter

and, poking around, we also discovered food, although it was barely edible. It consisted of strings of onions, such as the blue-jerseyed men from across the sea sometimes brought to Wherton, but these were withered and dry, in some cases rotten. They might have been brought here by the workers at the last picking, though it was hard to see why they should have been abandoned. At any rate, they stayed the protests of our bellies to some extent. We sat in the doorway of the hut, chewing on them, and watched the light fade behind the line of hills. It was peaceful and, even with a supper of stale and wilted onions and the prospect of a night on a hard clay floor, I felt more contented than I had done since leaving the castle. The things that had disturbed me seemed to fade with distance. And we were doing well. In a few more days we should be within reach of the mountains.

Then Henry went around to the other side of the hut and, a moment later, called to us to come, too. He did not need to draw our attention to it. The Tripod stood anchored to the hillside, not much more than half a mile away.

Henry said, "Do you think it's the same one?"

I said, "It wasn't in sight when we came up to the hut. I looked over that way."

Henry said uneasily, "Of course, they all look alike."

"We must go on," said Beanpole. "It may be accidental, but it is better not to take chances."

We abandoned the hut, and toiled on up the hill. We lay in a ditch that night, and I did not sleep well, though fortunately the rain held off. But I doubt if I should have slept at all in the hut, aware of the monstrous sentinel outside.

The Tripod was not in sight when we set out in the morning, but not long after we stopped at midday, it, or another, heaved across the brow of the hill behind us, and halted at much the same distance. I felt my legs trembling.

Beanpole said, "We must lose it."

"Yes," Henry said, "but how?"

"Perhaps we help it," Beanpole said, "by staying in the open."

Ahead of us lay fields, some with vines, others

with different crops. To the left, a little off our course, there were trees—the edge, it appeared, of a forest which seemed to extend over the folds of land beyond.

"We will see," Beanpole said, "if it can watch us through leaves and branches."

We found a field planted with turnips before we entered the forest, and filled our packs with these, realizing there might be small chance of provender ahead. But it was an immense relief to be concealed: the green ceiling was thick over our heads. We saw only occasional fragments of the sky, the sun not at all.

Traveling was more difficult, of course, and more exhausting. In places, the trees were very thick, and there were others where the undergrowth was so tangled that we were obliged to find a way around rather than force a path through. At first, we half expected to hear the Tripod crashing through the forest behind us, but as the hours went by with nothing but ordinary woodland noises—birds, the chatter of a squirrel, a distant grunting that was most likely a wild pig—we grew confident that, whether or not we had been right in thinking we were being pursued, we had put the idea out of the question now.

We stayed in the forest that night, ending our day a little early on the lucky chance of coming across a woodman's hut. There was kindling, and I made a fire, while Henry took a couple of wire snares that were hanging on the wall, and set them at the entrances to some rabbit holes nearby. He caught one, when it came out for its night run, and we skinned it and roasted it over the burning logs. We ate the rabbit by itself. There were still some turnips left, but by this time we were heartily sick of them.

The next morning, we headed for open country again, and reached it in a little over an hour. There was no sign of a Tripod, and we set off in good spirit, over land which was more wild than culti- vated, having a few meadows grazing cows and goats, and occasional patches of potatoes and the like, but mostly moorland—scrub grass and bushes, includ- ing one that bore great quantities of a blue berry with a sweet and delicate taste. We gorged ourselves on these, and filled our packs with little potatoes.

Steadily the land rose, and equally steadily grew barer. The forest had fallen away to the east, but there were clumps of pine which thickened to form a wood. We walked through its soft silence, where even bird song was hushed and far away, and came toward evening to the crest of a ridge, below which, for a hundred yards or more, the pines had been felled not long since: the axe-scarred stumps gleamed white, and many of the trees were still lying where they had fallen, waiting to be dragged away.

It was a vantage point. We could see down the slope of land, over the dark green tops of the standing trees, to other higher hills. And beyond them, so remote, so tiny seeming, and yet majestic, their tops white, flushed with pink by the setting sun, pressed against the deep blue of the sky—I marveled to think that that was snow . . . At last we were in sight of the White Mountains.

Henry said, sounding dazed, "They must be miles high."

"I suppose so."

I felt better, looking at them. In themselves they

seemed to challenge the metal monsters who strode, unchecked and omnipotent, over the lower lands. I could believe now, fully believe, that men might shelter beneath them, and remain free. I was thinking about this when Beanpole moved suddenly beside me.

"Listen!"

I heard it, and turned. It was behind us, and a long way off, but I knew what it was: the crash and splinter of wood under the massive impact of metal—the great feet stamping their way up through the pine wood. Then they stopped. We could glimpse it through a small gap in the trees, etched against the sky.

Beanpole said, "We have not been in sight all the afternoon. We are not in sight now. And yet it knows we are here."

I said, with a sick heart, "It could be coincidence."

"Twice, yes. A third time, even. But not when the same thing happens, again and again. It is following us, and it does not need to see us. As a dog will follow a scent."

Henry said, "That's impossible!"

"Where nothing else explains, the impossible is true."

"But why follow? Why not come and pick us up?"

"How can one tell what is in their minds?" Beanpole asked. "It may be that it is interested in what we do—where we go."

All the elation of a minute earlier had faded. The White Mountains existed. They might provide us with refuge. But they were still a journey of many days away, the Tripod no more than a few giant's strides.

Henry asked, "What are we going to do?"

"We must think," Beanpole said. "So far it is content with following us. That gives us time. But perhaps not much time."

We set off down the slope. The Tripod did not move from its position, but we were no longer under any illusion about that. We slogged on in a dispirited silence: I tried to think of some way of shaking it off, but the harder I concentrated the more hopeless it seemed. I hoped the other two were having better success. Surely Beanpole could think of something.

But he had not thought of anything by the time

we stopped for the night. We slept beneath the pines. It stayed dry and, even at this height, was fairly warm, and the bed of needles, inches thick it seemed from the long years of shedding, was softer than anything I had slept on since the castle. But there was not much consolation in that.

NINE

WE FIGHT A BATTLE

T HE MORNING WAS GLOOMY, MATCHING OUR mood; the pines were enshrouded in a thin gray cold mist, which brought us to shivering wakefulness while there was still barely enough light to see our way. We stumbled through the trees, trying to warm ourselves by our activity, and gnawing on raw potatoes as we went. We had not been able to see much of the valley the night before, and could see nothing now. It grew more light, but visibility was limited by the mist. There was a circle of a few yards, and after that the trunks of trees melted into the surrounding monochrome.

Of course, we saw nothing of the Tripod. Nor did we hear anything: the only sound was the sound of our own progress and that, over the carpet of pine needles, was so quiet that it could not have carried much beyond the field of view, if as far. A day earlier, this would have been heartening, but we could not pretend that it made any difference that, for the present, our pursuer was out of sight and hearing. It had been so for well over twenty-four hours, and then had come, through the trackless forest of pines, to stand over us.

We came out of the pines into wet grass which soaked our feet and the lower part of our legs. It was very cold. We had been setting a faster pace than usual, but the exercise had not warmed us. I was shivering, my teeth chattering a little. We did not talk much, and what we said was bare and unhopeful. There was no point in asking Beanpole if he had thought of a way out. One only had to look at his long miserable face, pinched by the cold, to see that he had not.

The valley bottomed out, and we bore to the west. The map had showed us that if we followed it for some miles we would find an easier ascent. We were continuing to go by the map automatically, for want of anything better. We heard the lonely gurgle and splash and chatter of water, and found a river and followed it. We had been traveling for some hours, and I was as chilled and wretched as at the start, and a good deal more hungry. There was no sign of food or life here.

Then, gradually, the mist lifted. The dirty gray turned whiter, became translucent, gleamed with silver, here and there admitted a shaft of brightness that dazzled briefly on the tumbling surface of the water before snuffing out. Our spirits lifted with it, to some extent, and when the sun appeared, first as a thin silver disc and at last as an orb of burning gold, we felt almost cheerful by comparison. I told myself that perhaps we had been wrong in thinking the Tripod had some magical way of tracking us. Perhaps its means of following us had been through senses—sight, hearing—which were only in degree better than our own. And if that were so, might it not in the long trek through the mist have lost us? It was not a rational optimism, but it made me feel better. The last of the mists trailed away into the distance, and we were traversing a broad sunlit valley, with the high ground on either side draped in white cloud. Birds were singing. Apart from them, we were entirely alone.

Until I heard a distant crackling far up on the hillside, and looked there and saw it, half-veiled in cloud but hideously real.

In the afternoon we found a clump of horseradish, and pulled the roots up and ate them. The taste was bitter and fiery, but it was food. We had left the valley, starting a climb up long but fairly moderate slopes of rough scrubland, and the Tripod was out of view again. But not out of mind. The feeling of hopelessness, of being caught in a trap which in due course must close, continually strengthened. I had followed the fox hunts on foot back at Wherton, but I would have had no stomach for them after this. Even the sun, which beat down more warmly than ever out of a clear sky, could not cheer me. When, with its rays slanting low from the west, Beanpole called a halt, I dropped on to the grass, empty and exhausted. The other two, after resting a while, stirred themselves and began foraging, but I did not move. I lay on my back, eyes closed against the light, hands clasped under the back of my neck. I still did not move when they came back, arguing about whether one could eat snakes—Henry had seen one but failed to kill it—and whether, anyway, they were hungry enough to eat it raw since there was no kindling for a fire. I kept my eyes shut when Henry, in quite a different, sharper voice, said:

"What's that?"

It would not, I was sure, be anything that mattered. Beanpole said something, in a lower voice, which I did not catch. They were whispering together. I kept my closed eyes on the sun, which would soon be gone behind the hills. They whispered again. Then Beanpole said:

"Will."

"Yes."

"Your shirt is torn, under the arm."

I said, "I know. I ripped it on a thorn bush coming up from the river."

"Look at me, Will." I opened my eyes, and saw

him standing over me, looking down. There was a strange look on his face. "What is it you have, under your arm?"

I got into a sitting position. "Under my arm? What are you talking about?"

"You do not know?" I had put my right hand under my left arm. "No, the other one."

I used my left arm this time, feeling into my armpit. I touched something whose texture was not the texture of flesh, but smoother and harder— something like a small metal button, on whose surface my fingertips traced faint corrugations, a kind of mesh. I craned my head around, trying to look at it, but could not. It seemed to melt into my skin, with no clear division between them. I looked up, and saw the other two watching me.

"What is it?"

"It is the metal of the Caps," Beanpole said. "It grows into the skin, as the Caps do."

"The Tripod . . ." I said. "When it caught me, outside the castle, do you think . . . ?"

I did not need to finish the sentence. Their faces showed me what they thought. I said wildly:

"You don't think I've been guiding it—that I'm under its control?"

Henry said, "It's been following since a few days after you caught up with us. We can't throw it off, can we? Have you got a better way of accounting for it?"

I stared at him. The mystery of the Tripod's ability to find us, time after time, and the mystery of the small metal button, somehow welded to my body— they could not be separated; they must belong together. And yet my mind was my own: I was no traitor. I had the same certainty of that as I had of my very existence. But how could I prove it? There was no way I could see.

Henry turned to Beanpole. "What are we going to do with him?"

Beanpole said, "We must think carefully, before we do anything."

"We haven't got time for that. We know he's one of them. He's been sending messages to it with his mind. He's probably sent one saying he's been found out. It may be coming after us right now."

"Will told us of the Tripod," Beanpole said.

"That it caught him, and released him again—that he was unconscious and could remember nothing. If his mind had been a servant of the Tripods, would he have said those things? And would he not have taken care, when his shirt was torn, rather than lie so that we could see it? Moreover, it is very small, not like the Caps, and not near the brain."

"But it is tracking us through him!"

"Yes, I believe so. The compass—it points to the north, because there must be much iron there. If you bring other iron near, it will point to that. One cannot see or feel the thing that makes it do this. The Tripod caught him, going away from the castle, when everyone there was asleep. He was un-Capped, but it did not Cap him. Maybe it was curious about what he would do, where he was going. And put this thing on him which it could follow, like a needle on a compass."

It made sense: I was sure what he said was true. I could feel the button under my arm with every small movement I made—not hurting, but I knew it was there. Why had I not felt it before? The same thought must have occurred to Henry.

"But he must have known about it," he said. "A thing like that."

"Perhaps not. Do you have in your country . . . people who make show . . . with animals, those who swing through the air from bars, strong men, and such?"

"Circuses," Henry said. "I saw one once."

"One that came to my town had a man who did strange things. He told people to sleep, and to obey his commands, and they did as he ordered, even doing things which made them look foolish. Sometimes the commands lasted for a time. A sailor with a crippled hip walked with no limp for a week—afterward, the pain and the limp returned."

"I can feel it now," I said.

"We have shown it to you," Beanpole said. "It may be that breaks the command."

Henry said impatiently, "None of this alters the facts. The Tripod can trace him through that thing, and can pick us up along with him."

I saw his point. I said, "There's only one thing to do."

"What is that?" Beanpole asked.

"If we separate, and I go a different way from you—it can follow me still, but you will be all right."

"A different way to the White Mountains? But you will still lead it there. Most likely, that is what it wishes."

I shook my head. "I won't go there. I'll double back."

"And be caught again. And Capped?"

I remembered the moment of being plucked from Aristide's back, the ground shrinking beneath me. I hoped I was not going white with the fear I felt. I said, "It will have to catch me first."

"It will catch you," Beanpole said. "You have no chance of escaping."

I said, trying not to think of what it entailed, "I can lead it away, at least."

There was a silence. It was, as I had said, the only thing to do, and they were bound to agree with it. There was no need, really, for them to say anything. I got to my feet, turning away from their faces. Beanpole said, "Wait."

"For what?"

"I said that we must think. I have been thinking. This thing under your arm—it is small, and though it is fastened to the skin I do not think it goes far beneath."

He paused. Henry said, "Well?"

Beanpole looked at me. "It is clear of the big vein. But it will hurt if we cut it out."

I had not seen what he was driving at, and hope, when I did, made me dizzy.

"Do you think you can?"

"We can try."

I began stripping off my shirt. "Let's not waste time then!"

Beanpole was not to be hurried. He made me lie down, with my arm up, and explored the button and the skin around it with his fingers. I wanted him to get on with it, but I was in his hands, and realized there was no point in showing impatience. At last, he said:

"Yes, it will hurt. I will do it as quickly as I can, but you will need something to bite on. And, Henry—you must hold his arm out, so that he cannot draw it back."

He gave me the leather strap of his pack to hold between my teeth; I felt the sour harsh taste of it on my tongue. The knife was one he had picked up in the great-city. It had a good edge, having been protected by grease, and he had spent some time sharpening it since then. It could not be too sharp for my liking. At a word from Beanpole, Henry took my arm, and stretched it out and back behind me. I was lying on my left hip, my face toward the ground. An ant scurried along and disappeared between blades of grass. Then there was the weight of Beanpole squatting over me, his left hand feeling again at the flesh under my arm, outlining the shape of the button. I was making a trial bite at the leather when he made the first cut, and my whole body jerked and I very nearly pulled my hand free from Henry's grasp. The pain was excruciating.

It was followed by another slash, and another. I tried to concentrate on the leather strap, through which my teeth seemed to be almost meeting. I was sweating so much that I felt drops rolling down the side of my face, and I saw one splash in the dust. I wanted to cry to him to stop, to let me have a rest from the pain, and was on the point of spitting the strap out to be able to speak when a new jab made me bite it again, and the side of my tongue with it. There was the hot salty taste of blood in my mouth, and tears in my eyes. Then, from a great distance, I heard him say: "You can let go now," and my hand and arm were free. The pain was furious still, but mild compared with what it had been a little earlier. Beanpole got up from me, and I started to drag myself to my feet. I had to move my arm to do so, and felt sick with what it did to me.

"As I thought," Beanpole said, "it is on the surface only. Observe."

I got rid of the gag, and looked at what he was holding in his hand. It was silvery gray, about half an inch in diameter, thicker in the center and tapering toward the edge. It was solid, but gave the impression of hundreds of tiny wires just below the surface. Attached to it were the bloody scraps of my flesh, which Beanpole had cut away.

Beanpole poked the button with his finger.

"It is curious," he said. "I would like to study this. It is a pity we must leave it."

His gaze was one of dispassionate interest. Henry, who was also looking, had a greenish tinge to his face. Staring at the gobbets of flesh adhering, nausea rose in me again, and this time I had to turn away to be sick. When I recovered, Beanpole was still staring at the button.

Gasping, I said, "Throw it away, and let's get going. The farther we are from here, the better."

He nodded reluctantly, and dropped it in the grass. He said to me, "Your arm—does it hurt much?"

"I wouldn't care to bowl fast for the next hour or two."

"Bowl fast?"

"In cricket. It's a game we play in our country. Oh, never mind. Let's get a move on. It will take my mind off it."

"There is a herb which heals wounds. I will look for it on the way."

A good deal of blood had flowed and was still flowing down my side. I had been mopping it up with my shirt, and I now rolled the shirt up into a ball, wadded it under my arm, and walked with it in that position. My hopeful suggestion that traveling would take my mind off the pain did not work out very well. It went on hurting just as much, if not more. But I was rid of the Tripod's button, and each jolting step left it farther behind.

We were continuing to climb over rough, but mostly open country. The sun was setting on our right; on the other side our long shadows were almost abreast of us. We were not talking, in my case because I was too occupied with gritting my teeth. It was, if one were in the mood for appreciating it, a lovely and peaceful evening. Calm and still. No sound, except . . .

We stopped, and listened. My heart seemed to contract, and for a moment the pain was blotted out by the greater power of fear. It came from behind, faint but seeming to grow louder every instant: the hideous warbling ululation which we had heard in the cabin of the *Orion*—the hunting call of the Tripods.

Seconds later it was in sight, coming around the base of the hill and, unmistakably, climbing toward us. It was some miles away, but coming on fast—much faster, I thought, than its usual rate of progress.

Henry said, "The bushes . . ."

He did not need to say any more; we were all three running. What he had indicated offered one of the few bits of cover on the hillside, the only one within reasonable reach. It was a small thicket of bushes, growing to about shoulder height. We flung ourselves in among them, burrowed into the center, and crouched down there.

I said, "It can't still be after me. Can it?"

"The button," Beanpole said. "It must be that cutting it out gave an alarm. So it has come after you, and this time hunting."

"Did it see us, do you think?" Henry asked.

"I do not know. It was far away, and the light is poor."

In fact, the sun had gone down; the sky above our hiding place was drained of gold, a darker blue. But still terrifyingly clear—much lighter than it had been the morning I had left the castle. I tried to console myself with the thought that I had been much nearer to it, also. The howling was louder and closer. It must have reached and passed the place where Beanpole had operated on me. Which meant . . .

I felt the ground shiver, and again and again with still greater force. Then one of the Tripod's legs plunged across the blue, and I saw the hemisphere, black against the arc of sky, and tried to dig myself down into the earth. At that moment the howling stopped. In the silence I heard a different whistling sound of something whipping terribly fast through the air and, glancing fearfully, saw two or three bushes uprooted and tossed away.

Beside me, Beanpole said, "It has us. It knows we are here. It can pull the bushes out till we are plainly seen."

"Or kill us, pulling them out," Henry said. "If that thing hits you . . ."

I said, "If I showed myself . . ."

"No use. It knows there are three."

"We could run different ways," Henry said. "One of us might get clear."

I saw more bushes sail through the air, like confetti. You do not get used to fear, I thought; it grips you as firmly every time. Beanpole said, "We can fight it."

He said it with a lunatic calm, which made me want to groan. Henry said, "What with? Our fists?"

"The metal eggs." He had his pack open already, and was rummaging in it. The Tripod's tentacle whistled down again. It was ripping the bushes up systematically. A few more passes—half a dozen at most—would bring it to us. "Perhaps these were what our ancestors used, to fight the Tripods. Perhaps that is why they were in the underground Shmand-Fair— they went out from there to fight them."

I said, "And they lost! How do you think . . . ?"

He had got the eggs out. "What else is there?"

Henry said, "I threw mine away. They were too much trouble to carry."

The tentacle sliced into the bushes, and this time we were spattered with earth as it pulled them up. Beanpole said: "There are four."

He handed one each to Henry and me. "I will take the others. If we pull out the rings, count five, then stand up and throw. At the leg that is nearest. The hemisphere is too high."

This time I saw the tentacle *through* the bushes as it scooped up more. Beanpole said, "Now!"

He pulled the rings from his eggs, and Henry did the same. I had taken mine in my left hand, and I needed to transfer it to the right. As I did so, pain ripped my armpit again, and I dropped it. I was fumbling on the ground to pick it up when Beanpole said, "Now!" again. They scrambled to their feet, and I grabbed the last egg, ignoring the pain of the moment, and got up with them. I ripped out the ring just as they threw.

The nearest foot of the Tripod was planted on the slope, thirty yards or so above us. Beanpole's first throw was wild—he did not get within ten yards of his target. But his second throw, and Henry's, were close to the mark. One of them hit metal, with a clang that we could hear. Almost at once they exploded. There were three nearly simultaneous bangs, and fountains of earth and dust spouted into the air.

But they did not obscure one plain fact: the eggs had done no damage to the Tripod. It stood as firmly as before, and the tentacle was swishing down, this time directly toward us. We started to run, or rather, in my case, prepared to. Because before I could move, it had me around the waist.

I plucked at it with my left hand, but it was like trying to bend a rock. It held me with amazing precision, tight but not crushing, and lifted me as I might lift a mouse. Except that a mouse could bite, and I could do nothing against the hard gleaming surface that held me. I was lifted up, up. The ground shrank below me, and with it the figures of Beanpole and Henry. I saw them darting away like ants. I was steeplehigh, higher. I looked up, and saw the hole in the side of the hemisphere. And remembered the iron egg still clutched in my right hand.

How long was it since I had pulled the ring out? I had forgotten to count in my fear and confusion. Several seconds—it could not be long before it exploded. The tentacle was swinging me inwards now. The hole was forty feet away, thirty-five, thirty. I braced myself back, straining against the encircling band. Pain leapt in my arm again, but I ignored it. I hurled the egg with all my strength, and what accuracy I could muster. I thought at first that I had missed, but the egg hit the edge of the opening and ricocheted inside. The tentacle continued to carry me forward. Twenty feet, fifteen, ten . . .

Although I was nearer, the explosion was not as loud as the others had been, probably because it took place inside the hemisphere. There was just a dull, rather hollow bang. Despair came back: that was my last chance gone. But at that instant I felt the tentacle holding me relax and fall away.

I was three times the height of a tall pine; my bones would shatter when I hit the ground. I clutched desperately at the thing against which, a few seconds earlier, I had been struggling. My hands gripped the metal, but I was falling, falling. I looked down, and closed my eyes as the earth rushed up to meet me. And then there was a jerk which almost tore me from my hold, and the falling stopped. My feet shivered, only a few inches above the ground. All I had to do was let go, and step down.

The others came to me. We stared up, in awe, at the Tripod. It stood there, tilted slightly but upright. From where we stood it showed no sign of damage. But its tentacle drooped like a dead snake. Our tormentor would not torment us again.

TEN

THE WHITE MOUNTAINS

BEANPOLE SAID, "I DO NOT KNOW IF IT COULD tell others before it died, but I think we had better not stay here."

Henry and I quickly agreed. For my part, even though I knew it was dead, I still, irrationally, feared it. I had a vision of it toppling, crushing us beneath its stupendous weight. I wanted desperately to get away from this place.

"If others come," Beanpole said, "they will search the surrounding part. The more distant we are before that happens, the better for us."

We set off up the hill, running. We ran until we

were straining for breath, hearts pounding deliriously, leg muscles tortured with fatigue, and still staggered on. My arm was hurting a lot, but after a time I felt it less than I felt the other aches and pains. Once I fell, and it was an exquisite pleasure just to lie there, panting but not moving, my face pressed against grass and powdery earth. The others helped me up, and I was partly angry as well as grateful.

It took us about half an hour to get to the top. Beanpole stopped then, and we stopped with him—I do not think I could have gone more than a few more yards, anyway, before falling again. And this time no help would have got me to my feet. I gulped in breath, which hurt me but which I had to have. Gradually the tightness in my chest eased, and I could breathe without pain.

I looked down the long slope up which we had come. Darkness was falling, but I could still see the Tripod there. Was it really possible that I had killed it? I could begin to appreciate the enormity of what I had done, not so much with pride as with wonder. The unchallenged, impregnable masters of the earth—and my right hand had smashed one to death.

I thought I knew how David had felt, when he saw Goliath topple in the dust of the valley of Elah.

Beanpole said, "Look."

His voice did not generally tell one much, but there was alarm in it. I said, "Where?"

"To the west."

He pointed. In the far distance, something moved. A familiar hateful shape heaved itself over the skyline, followed by a second, and a third. They were a long way off yet, but the Tripods were coming.

We ran again, down the other side of the ridge. We lost sight of them at once, but that was small consolation, knowing they were in the next valley, and realizing the feebleness of the best speed we could manage in comparison with theirs. I hoped they would stay with the dead Tripod for some time, but doubted if they would. Seeking revenge for its destruction was more likely to be their immediate concern. I put my foot on uneven ground, stumbled, and came near falling. At least, it was dark and getting darker. Unless they had cat's eyes, it made our chances just a little better.

And we needed all the help we could get. There appeared to be no more cover in this valley than the last—less, because I could not see a single bush, let alone a clump of them. It was all rough grass, with outcroppings of stone. We rested against one of these when exhaustion finally halted us. Stars were out, but there was no moon: it would not rise for some hours. I was very glad of that.

No moon, but, above the ridge, a light in the sky, a light that moved, changing shape. A number of lights? I drew Beanpole's attention to it. He said,

"Yes. I have seen that."

"The Tripods?"

"What else?"

The light became beams, thrusting forward across the sky like arms. They shortened, and one of them swung in a stabbing arc across the sky, so that it pointed down instead of up. I could not see what lay behind the beam, but it was easy enough to imagine. The Tripod had come over the crest. The beams of light came from the hemispheres, and enabled them to see their way.

They were spaced out, a hundred yards or so

apart, and the beams of light swept the ground before and between them. They were traveling more slowly than I had seen a Tripod travel, but even so they were going faster than we could run. And were, as far as we knew, tireless. They made no sound, save for the dull thumping of their feet, and somehow this was more frightening than the howling of the other Tripod had been.

We ran, and rested, and ran again. Rather than endure the extra effort of scaling the far side, we followed the valley to the west. In the darkness we stumbled and fell over the uneven ground, bruising ourselves. Behind us, the light followed, relentlessly weaving to and fro. In one pause, we saw that the Tripods had split up, one going up the other side of the valley and another marching to the east. But the third was coming our way, and gaining on us.

We heard a stream and, on Beanpole's suggestion, made for it. Since the three of them were apparently searching in different directions, it did not seem likely that they were following a scent, but there was a chance that they might, or might follow our tracks through grass and where the earth was soft. We got into the stream, and splashed our way along. It was only a few feet wide, luckily quite shallow and with an even, pebbly bed. The wonderful leather boots that had been made for me by the cobbler at the castle would not be improved by the soaking, but I had more pressing things to think about.

We paused again. The stream splashed against our legs, just above our ankles. I said, "We can't go on like this. It will have reached us in another quarter of an hour."

Henry said, "What else can we do?"

"There's only one Tripod now. Its light covers just about the whole of the valley floor, and perhaps a little of the sides. If we make a break for it, up the slope—it might miss us and go on past."

"Or it might trace our tracks out of the stream, and follow us."

"We should take the risk. We have no chance at all this way." He did not say anything. "What do you think, Beanpole?"

"I?" he said. "I think it is too late already. Look ahead."

Along the valley there was a light, which brightened and, as I watched, became a beam. We gazed at it in silence and despair. Then another light appeared above the ridge which I had suggested our climbing, twisted in the air, and arced down. And there were other lights, less distinct above the opposite slope. It was no longer a question of one Tripod, remorselessly gaining on us from behind. They were here in force, and all around.

"Should we scatter?" Henry suggested. "I suppose we might have more chance separated than together."

I said, "No. The same chance. None at all, that is."

"I think I'm going to try," Henry said. "The way it is, once they spot one, they've got us all."

Beanpole said, "Wait."

"For what? A few minutes and it will be too late."

"That rock, there."

Visibility was better, because of the light diffused from the Tripods' beams. We could see each other, as though in dim moonlight, and a little of our surroundings. Beanpole pointed down the stream. Some twenty yards ahead, there was a shadowy ridge of rock, more than head high.

"It may give some cover," Beanpole said.

I doubted that. We might flatten ourselves against it, but the beams would still catch us. But I had nothing better to offer. Beanpole splashed off along the stream, and we splashed after him. The course of the stream ran right beside the rock, which I saw had diverted its course to some extent. The reef was about thirty feet long. Its upper part was smooth and flat with a gentle backward slope, providing no protection at all. But the lower part . . .

Some time in the past the stream had been stronger and more turbulent than it was now, and its fierceness had worn away a band of stone at the base. We bent down, exploring it with our hands. At its maximum the crevice was not more than two feet high, and about as deep; but it seemed to run the length of the rock. Two more beams appeared on the northern escarpment of the valley, and one of them was flicking far ahead, making spots of light that darted perilously near to where we stood. There was no room for delay. We snuggled ourselves into the crevice, in line, head to toe—Beanpole, then Henry, with myself at the end. My right arm was against rock, but my left side felt terribly exposed. I tried to force myself farther in, even though it hurt my arm to do so. If I lifted my head just a fraction, my forehead touched the stone overhang. The sound of my breathing seemed loud in this confinement.

Beanpole whispered, "No talking. We must stay here quietly. For an hour, perhaps."

I watched the scene outside brighten, as the Tripods came nearer, and heard the thump, heavier and heavier, of their feet. Eventually I could see light reflected from the surface of the stream farther up. Then, directly in front of my face, night became day, and I could see small stones, blades of grass, a beetle frozen into immobility, all with tremendous clarity. And the ground shook as the foot of a Tripod slammed down only a few yards from us. I pressed myself tightly against the rock. It was going to be a long hour.

A long hour, indeed. All night the beams of light played across the hills, advancing and retreating, crossing and recrossing the ground. Dawn broke at last, but the hunt did not stop. The Tripods came and went in a constant traffic: allowing for the same ones passing over us time after time, there must still have been dozens of them.

But they had not seen us, and as the hours wore slowly on we became more and more confident that they would not. Even in daylight, our cleft must be invisible from the height of the hemispheres. But by the same token, we dared not leave its shelter. We lay there in increasing discomfort and boredom and hunger, seasoned in my case with pain. My arm began to hurt very badly, and there were times when I thought I would make my lip bleed with biting on it, and I felt tears come to my eyes and run down my cheeks.

By midday, the intensity of the search had begun to slacken. There were periods of as long as five or ten minutes in which we dared to creep out and stretch our legs, but always they ended with the distant sight of another Tripod, and every now and then a troop of them would come stamping through the valley. We could not go far from the crevice; there was no other cover of any kind.

Day drifted into dusk, and dusk into night, and

there were the beams of light again. There were not so many as before, but there was never a time that one could not see them either in the valley or lighting the sky beyond the heights. Occasionally I dozed off into sleep, but never for long. The awareness of rock directly above my face was smothering—I was cold and aching, and my arm was burning and throbbing. Once I woke up, moaning with the pain of it. Surely they would go with daybreak? I watched the sky, greedy for the first inkling of natural light. It came at last, a gray cloudy dawn, and we emerged, shivering, and looked about us. There had been no beams of light for half an hour or more, and there were none now. But five minutes later we scurried back into hiding, as another Tripod lurched up the valley.

So it went on, all that morning and long into the afternoon. I was too miserable, dazed with hunger and pain, to pay attention to anything but the business of enduring from one moment to the next, and I do not think the others were in much better shape. When, toward evening, a lengthening period without Tripods made it seem that the search might finally be off, we found it difficult to take it in. We came out of the cleft but for a couple of hours at least sat huddled by the stream, watching for signs of their return.

Darkness was falling by the time we made up our minds to go on, and it was an indication of our wretchedness and confusion that we should have done so. We were weak from hunger, and utterly weary. A mile or two farther on, we collapsed and lay all night in the open, with no hope of concealment if the Tripods came back. But they did not, and dawn showed us an empty valley, flanked by silent hills.

The days that followed were hard. For me, particularly, because my arm had festered. In the end, Beanpole cut it again, and I am afraid I was less stoical this time, and shrieked with pain. Afterward Beanpole put some of the healing herbs, which he had found, on the wound, binding them in place with a bandage made from the tail of my shirt, and Henry said he knew it must have been pretty agonizing: he would have shrieked a lot more. I was more glad of his kindness than I would have expected.

We found a few roots and berries, but we were hungry all the time and we shivered in our thin clothes, especially during the nights. The weather had changed. There was a lot of cloud and a cold breeze from the south. We reached high ground, from where it should have been possible to see the White Mountains, but there was no sign of them—only an empty gray horizon. There were moments when I felt that what we had seen before had been a mirage rather than a reality.

Then we came down into a plain, and there was a stretch of water so immense that one could not see its end: the Great Lake of the map. The country was rich and fertile. We were able to get more food, and better, and with the satisfaction of hunger, our spirits began to pick up. Beanpole's herbs, I found, had worked; my arm was healing cleanly now.

One morning, after a good night's sleep among hay in a barn, we awoke to find the sky once more blue, and all things bright and light. There were the hills which fringed the plain to the south, and beyond them, splendid and looking so close that one almost felt one could reach out and touch them, the snowy peaks of the White Mountains.

• • •

Of course, they were nothing like as close as they seemed. There were miles of plain still, and then the foothills. But at least we could see them, and we set out in good heart. We had been traveling for an hour, and Henry and I were making jokes about Beanpole's gigantic steam-kettle, when he stopped us. I thought the jokes had annoyed him, but then felt, as he had already done, the earth quiver beneath our feet.

They were coming from the northeast, from our left and behind—two Tripods, moving fast and heading directly for us. I looked around desperately, but knew what I would see. The land was green and flat, without a tree or rock, a hedge or ditch, and the nearest farmhouse was half a mile away.

Henry said, "Shall we run for it?"

"Run where?" Beanpole asked. "It is no good."

His voice was flat. If he recognized it was hopeless, I thought, then it was hopeless indeed. In a minute or two they would be on us. I looked away from them to the gleaming battlements of white. To have come so far, endured so much, and to lose with our goal in sight—it was unfair.

The earth shook more violently. They were a

hundred yards away, fifty . . . They marched side by side, I saw, and their tentacles were doing strange things, probing and retreating from each other, describing elaborate patterns in the air. And something moved between and above them, a golden something that flashed with brightness, tossed to and fro against the blue of sky.

They were on us. I waited for a tentacle to reach down and seize me, conscious less of fear than of a futile anger. A great foot slammed down a few yards from us. And then they were past, and going away, and my legs felt as though they were buckling. Beanpole said, in wonder, "They did not see us. Because they were too concerned with each other? Some ritual of mating, perhaps? But they are machines. What then? It is a puzzle to which I would like the answer."

He was welcome, I thought, both to the puzzle and its answer. All I could feel was the weakness of relief.

A long, difficult, and dangerous journey, Ozymandias told me. So it proved. And with a hard life at the journey's end. He was right in that, too. We have nothing in the way of luxury, and would not want it if we could: minds and bodies must be kept taut and trim for the tasks that lie ahead.

But there are wonders, of which our new home itself is the greatest. We live not only among the White Mountains but inside one of them. For the ancients built a Shmand-Fair here, too—six miles long, rising a mile high through a tunnel hewn out of solid rock. Why they did it, for what great purpose, we cannot tell; but now, with new tunnels carried still farther into the mountain's heart, it provides us with a stronghold. Even when we came to it, in summer, there was snow and ice around the opening to the main tunnel, and it emerges to a place that looks over a river of ice, inching its way down between frozen peaks to be lost in the distance. But inside the mountain, the air is no more than cool, protected as we are by the thick layers of rock.

There are viewing points where one can look out from the side of the mountain. Sometimes I go to one of these and stare down into the green sunlit valley far below. I can see villages, tiny fields, roads, the pinhead specks of cattle. Life looks warm there, and easy, compared with the harshness of rock and ice by which we are surrounded. But I do not envy the valley people their ease.

For it is not quite true to say that we have no luxuries. We have two: freedom, and hope. We live among men whose minds are their own, who do not accept the dominion of the Tripods and who, having endured in patience for long enough, are even now preparing to carry the war to the enemy.

Our leaders keep their counsel, and we are only newcomers and boys—we could not expect to know what the projects are, or what our part in them may be. But we shall have a part, that is certain. And another thing is certain, too: in the end we shall destroy the Tripods, and free men will enjoy the goodness of the earth.

WILL'S BATTLE AGAINST THE TRIPODS CONTINUES:

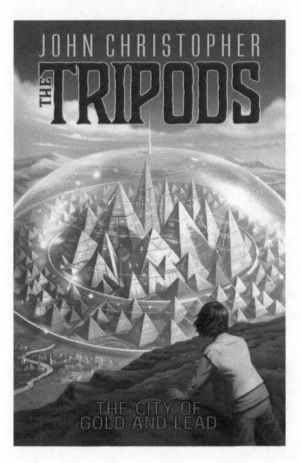

EVEN WHEN WE FIRST CAME TO THE WHITE
Mountains, in summer, the upper reaches of the
Tunnel looked out over fields of snow and ice;
but at the lower end there were rocks and grass and
a view of the glacier, stained brown with mud and
dripping into rivulets that ran down to the valley, far
far below. In September there was a fall of snow
which did not lie, but in the early days of October
the snow came again, more heavily, and this time
remained. The grip of winter tightened around us,
and it was to be more than half a year before those
white bony fingers unclenched.

Preparations for the siege had been made long before. Food had been stored, cattle and winter fodder taken into the inner recesses of the mountain which sheltered us. We did not need a great deal by way of heat, protected as we were by dozens, hundreds of yards of solid rock. Cool in summer, our deep caves were warm, by comparison, in winter. We wore furs when we were outside, but the rest of the time our normal clothing was enough.

Our lives were confined, but by no means idle. Reveille, for those of us in the training cadre, was at six, and was followed by half an hour's brisk exercise. After that came a simple breakfast, and then the first study period of the day, lasting three hours. There were more exercises before the midday meal, and in the afternoon exercise and instruction in our particular sports. If the weather were fine, this took place outside in the snow; otherwise in the Great Cavern. There was a second study period before supper, and afterward generally there was discussion among our seniors, to which we listened but in which we did not presume to join. It had one subject—the Tripods— and one purpose: their overthrow.

· · ·

The Tripods had been rulers of the earth for more than a hundred years. They governed simply and effectively, by dominating the minds of men. This was achieved through the Caps, meshes of silvery metal which fitted closely around the skull and were woven into the very flesh of their wearers. Capping occurred in one's fourteenth year, marking the point at which one ceased to be a child and became an adult. It was taken for granted, an expected, looked-for thing, attended by feasting and celebration.

A few months earlier I had seen my cousin Jack, a year older than myself, go through the ceremony, and had noticed the change in him afterward. I was to be Capped the following year. I had some misgivings, but I kept them private—no one talked much about Tripods and Cappings and, of course, no one ever queried the rightness of these things. Not, that is, until the Vagrant, Ozymandias, came to the little village where I lived.

The Vagrants were those for whom Capping had not worked properly. Their minds had refused to accept the conditioning of the Tripods and, in refusing, had been broken. They wandered from place to place, never resting long, and were looked after but pitied and disliked by normal Capped men and women. Now, though, I found myself more interested in them; particularly in the one who called himself Ozymandias, a big, red-haired, red-bearded man who sang strange songs, and spoke lines of poetry, and mixed sense and nonsense when he talked. Defying my parents, I invited him to come to the den which Jack and I had made just outside the village. He told me a strange story.

He was, in the first place, not really a Vagrant, but posing as such so that he could travel through the land, unchallenged and unremarked. The Cap he wore was a false one. He explained that the Tripods were enemies of men, not benefactors, invaders, perhaps, from another world, and how, through Capping, minds which were just beginning to think for themselves were subdued and harnessed to the worship of their oppressors. He told me, too, that although the Tripods ruled the planet, there were a few places where free men survived, and that one of these was among the White Mountains, across the sea from

England far to the south. He asked me if I would be willing to make a difficult and dangerous journey there, and I said I would.

He himself traveled on in search of more recruits, but I did not go alone. Another cousin of mine, Henry, an old antagonist since before our school-days, saw me leaving the village and followed me. We crossed the sea together, and in the land called France found a third, Jean-Paul—whom we named Beanpole. Together we made our way south. It was as difficult and dangerous as Ozymandias had promised. Near the end, we fought a battle with a Tripod and, by luck and a weapon of the ancients which we found in the ruins of one of the great-cities, destroyed it.

So, at last, we reached the White Mountains.

There were eleven of us in the training cadre, being prepared for the first move in the counterattack against our enemies. It was a hard schooling, in body and mind alike, but we knew a little of the task before us, and how heavy the odds against success were. The discipline and hardship we had to endure might not shorten those odds by much, but every bit counted.

For we—or some of us—were to conduct a reconnaissance. We knew almost nothing of the Tripods—not even whether they were intelligent machines or vehicles for alien beings. We must know more before we could hope to fight them successfully; and there was only one way to get that knowledge. Some of us, one at least, must penetrate into the City of the Tripods, study them, and bring back information. The plan was this:

The City lay to the north, in the country of the Germans. Each year some of the newly Capped, chosen in different ways, were brought there to serve the Tripods. I had witnessed one such way at the Château de la Tour Rouge, when Eloise, the daughter of the Comte, had been made Queen of the Tournament. I had been horrified to learn that at the end of her brief reign she should want to be taken to be a slave of the enemy, and go gladly, thinking it an honor.

Among the Germans, it seemed, there were Games each summer, to which young men came from hundreds of miles away. The winners were feasted and made much of after which they, too, went to serve in the City. At the next Games, it was hoped, one of us might win, and gain admission. What would happen after that was unknown. Anyone who succeeded would have to rely on his wits, both in spying on the Tripods and in passing on what he had learned. The last part was likely to be the hardest. Because although scores, perhaps hundreds, went yearly into the City, not one had ever been known to come out.

One day the snow was melting at the foot of the Tunnel where we exercised, and a week later it lay only in isolated patches, and there was the green of grass, dotted with purple crocuses. The sky was blue, and sunlight flamed from the white peaks all round, burning our skins through the thin pure air. During a break we lay on the grass and looked down. Figures moved cautiously half a mile below, visible to us but taking cover from those who might look up from the valley. This was the first raiding party of the season, on its way to plunder the fat lands of the Capped.

I sat with Henry and Beanpole, a little apart from the rest. The lives of all those who lived in the mountains were closely knit, but this strand was a more tightly woven one. In the things we had endured, jealousies and enmities had worn away and been replaced by true comradeship. The boys in the cadre were our friends, but the bond between us three was special.

Beanpole said gloomily, "I failed at one meter seventy today."

He spoke in German; we had learned the language but needed to practice it. I said, "One goes off form. You'll improve again."

"I'm getting worse every day."

Henry said, "Rodrigo's definitely gone off. I beat him comfortably."

"It's all right for you."

Henry had been chosen as a long-distance runner, and Rodrigo was his chief rival. Beanpole was training for long and high jumping. I was one of two boxers. There were four sports altogether—the other was sprint running—and they had been arranged to produce a maximum of competitiveness. Henry had done well in his event from the start. And I myself was fairly confident, at any rate, as far as my opponent here was concerned. This was Tonio, a dark-skinned boy from the south, taller than I and with a longer reach, but not as quick. Beanpole, though, had grown increasingly pessimistic about his chances.

Henry reassured him, telling him he had heard the instructors saying he was coming on well. I wondered if it were true, or said for encouragement: the former, I hoped.

I said, "I asked Johann if it had been decided yet how many were to go."

Johann, one of the instructors, was squat and powerful, yellow-haired, with the look of a bad-tempered bull but amiable at heart. Henry asked, "What did he say?"

"He wasn't sure, but he thought four—the best from each group."

"So it could be us three, plus an extra," Henry said.

Beanpole shook his head. "I'll never do it."

"You will."

I said, "And the fourth?"

"It might be Fritz."

He did seem to be the best of the sprint runners,

as far as we could tell. He was German himself, and came from a place on the edge of a forest to the northeast. His chief rival was a French boy, Etienne, whom I preferred. Etienne was cheerful and talkative, Fritz tall, heavy, taciturn.

I said, "As long as we all come through."

"You two will," Beanpole said.

Henry leaped to his feet. "There's the whistle. Come on, Beanpole. Time to get back to work."

The seniors had their own tasks. Some were our instructors; others formed the raiding parties to keep us supplied with food. There were still others who studied the few books that had survived from olden days, and tried to relearn the skills and mysteries of our ancestors. Beanpole, whenever he had a chance, would be with them, listening to their talk and even putting up suggestions of his own. Not long after we met he had spoken—wildly, as I thought—about using a sort of gigantic kettle to push carriages without the need for horses. Something like this had been discovered, or rediscovered, here, though it would not yet work properly. And there were plans for more remarkable things: making light and heat through something which had been called electricity was one.

And at the head of all the groups there was one man, whose hands held all the threads, whose decisions were unquestioned. This was Julius.

He was close on sixty years old, a small man and a cripple. When he was a boy he had fallen into an ice crevasse and broken his thigh: it had been set badly and he walked with a limp. In those days, things had been very different in the White Mountains. Those who lived there had no purpose but survival, and their numbers were dwindling. It was Julius who thought of winning recruits from the world outside, from those not yet Capped, and who believed—and made others believe—that some day men would fight back against the Tripods, and destroy them.

It was Julius, too, who had worked out the enterprise for which we were being trained. And it was Julius who would make the final decision on which of us were chosen.

He came out one day to watch us. He was white-haired, red-cheeked like most of those who had lived all their lives in this sharp, clear air, and he leaned on a stick. I saw him, and concentrated hard on the bout in which I was engaged. Tonio feinted with his left, and followed up with a right cross. I made him miss, hammered a sharp right to his ribs and, when he came in again, landed a left to the jaw which sent him sprawling.

Julius beckoned, and I ran to where he stood. He said, "You are improving, Will."

"Thank you, sir."

"I suppose you are getting impatient to know which of you will be going to the Games?"

I nodded. "A little, sir."

He studied me. "When the Tripod had you in its grasp—do you remember how you felt? Were you afraid?"

I remembered. I said, "Yes, sir."

"And the thought of being in their hands, in their City—does that frighten you?" I hesitated, and he went on: "There are two sides to the choice, you know. We old ones may be able to judge your quickness and skill, of mind and body, but we cannot read your hearts."

"Yes," I admitted, "it frightens me."

"You do not have to go. You can be useful here." His pale blue eyes looked into mine. "No one need know if you prefer to stay."

I said, "I want to go. I can bear the thought of being in their hands more easily than of being left behind."

"Good." He smiled. "And you, after all, have killed a Tripod—something I doubt any other human being can claim. You know that they are not all-powerful. That is an asset, Will."

"Do you mean, sir . . . ?"

"I mean what I said. There are other considerations. You must go on working hard, and preparing, in case you are chosen."

Later I saw him talking to Henry. I thought it was probably much the same conversation as mine had been. I did not ask him, though, and he did not volunteer anything about it.

During the winter our diet, although adequate, had been very dull, the staple item dried and salted meat, which, however hard the cooks tried, remained stodgy and unappetizing. In the middle of April, though, a raiding party brought back half a dozen black-and-white cows, and Julius decreed that one should be killed and roasted. After the feast, he spoke to us. When he had been talking a few minutes I realized, the excitement almost suffocating me, that this, almost certainly, was the moment for announcing the names of those who were to make the attempt at penetrating the City of the Tripods.

He had a quiet voice, and I was with the other boys at the far end of the cave, but his words were clear. Everyone was listening, attentively and in silence. I glanced at Henry, on my right. In the flickering light, I thought he looked very confident. My own confidence was ebbing rapidly. It would be bitter if he went, and I were left.

First, Julius talked about the plan in general. For months those in the training cadre had been preparing for their task. They would have some advantage over competitors from lower lands, because it was known that men in higher altitudes developed stronger lungs and muscles than those who lived in the thicker air. But it had to be remembered that there would be hundreds of competitors, drawn from the best athletes all over the country. It might be that, for all their preparation, not one of our small band would wear a champion's belt. In that case, they must find their way back to the White Mountains, and try again, next year. Patience was as necessary as determination.

Contestants in the Games must be Capped, of course. That presented no great difficulty. We had Caps, taken from those killed in forays into the valleys, which could be molded to fit the skulls of the ones chosen. They would look like Caps, but they would give no orders. Here, though, a problem did present itself.

We who had never been Capped could not know just how men's minds were controlled by them. It might be that they simply fixed the wearers in an attitude of uncritical obedience, of devotion, to the Tripods. In that case, our spies only needed to put on the appearance of willing slaves. But there was the possibility that the Tripods could talk to the minds of the Capped through the Caps, without the need for speech. That, it was plain, would mean discovery, and either execution or Capping. The former was the better fate.

Not only for the individuals but for those who stayed behind. It had been objected—I wondered who had dared to object to a plan put forward by Julius—that this involved the risk of betraying our existence to the Tripods, of provoking them to bring their power to bear and crush us. The risk must be taken. We could not skulk forever in the mountains. Even if we hid in holes all the time, eventually they would ferret us out and exterminate us, like vermin. Our hope of survival lay in attack.

Now to the details of the plan:

The City of the Tripods lay hundreds of miles to the north. There was a great river which covered most of that distance. Barges plied up and down it in trade, and one of these was in the hands of our men. It would sail to a spot within easy reach of the place where the Games were held.

Julius paused, before going on.

It had been decided that three should be selected from the training cadre. Many things had to be taken into account: individual skill and strength, the likely level of competition in the event, the temperament of the person and his probable usefulness once he had penetrated the Tripods' stronghold. It had not been easy, but the choices had been made. Raising his voice slightly, he called.

"Stand up, Will Parker."

For all my hopes, the shock of hearing my own name unnerved me. My legs trembled as I got to my feet.

Julius said, "You have shown ability as a boxer, Will, and you have the advantage of being small and light in weight. Your training has been with Tonio, who would be in a heavier class at the Games, and this should help you.

"The doubt we had was about you yourself. You are impatient, often thoughtless, likely to rush into things without giving careful enough consideration to what may happen next. From that point of view, Tonio would have been better. But he is less likely to succeed at the Games, which is our first concern. A heavy responsibility may rest on you. Can we rely on you to do your utmost to guard against your own recklessness?"

I promised, "Yes, sir."

"Sit down, then, Will. Stand up, Jean-Paul Deliet."

I think I felt gladder about Beanpole than when my own name was called; perhaps because I was less confused and had been less optimistic. I had picked up his own gloom about his chances. So there would be three—the three of us who had journeyed together before, who had fought the Tripod on the hillside.

Julius said, "There were difficulties in your case, too, Jean-Paul. You are the best of our jumpers, but it is not sure that you are up to the standard that will be necessary to win at the Games. And there is the question of your eyesight. The contraption of lenses you invented—or rediscovered because they were common among the ancients—is something that passed as an eccentricity in a boy, but the Capped do not have such eccentricities. You must blunder through a world in which you will see less clearly than your fellows. If you get inside the City, you will not perceive things with the clarity that Will, for instance, would.

"But what you see, you may understand better. Your intelligence is an asset which outweighs the weakness of your eyes. You could be the most useful in bringing back to us what we have to know. Do you accept the task?"

Beanpole said, "Yes, sir."

"And so we come to the third choice, which was the easiest." I saw Henry looking pleased with himself, and was childish enough to feel a little resentment. "He is the most likely to succeed in his event, and the best equipped for what may follow.

"Fritz Eger—do you accept?"

I tried to speak to Henry, but he made it plain that he wanted to be left alone. I saw him again later on, but he was morose and uncommunicative. Then, the following morning, I happened to go to the lookout gallery, and found him there.

The main Tunnel had been built by the ancients to take horseless carriages up through the mountain to a point near the top, where the great glacier rolled away between snowy peaks to the southeast. We had no idea why they had done that, but there was a big house at the top, and a building with a domed roof of metal that had a vast telescope pointing at the sky, and a cave where strange figures were carved in ice. On the way up, there were galleries, from which one looked out and down, and the lowest of these showed a rich green valley, thousands of feet below, in which one could see roads like black thread, tiny houses, pinpoint cattle in miniature meadows. There was a telescope here, too, a small one fixed in the rock, but one of the lenses had been broken and it was useless.

Henry was leaning against the low wall of rock, and turned as I approached. I said awkwardly, "If you want me to go . . ."

"No." He shrugged. "It doesn't matter."

"I'm . . . sorry."

He managed a grin. "Not as sorry as I am."

"If we went to see Julius . . . I don't see why there shouldn't be four instead of three."

"I've already seen him."

"And there's no hope?"

"None. I'm the best of my group, but they don't think I'd stand much chance in the Games. Perhaps next year, if I keep at it."

"I don't see why you shouldn't *try* this year."

"I said that, too. He says even three is really too large a party to send out. So much more chance of being spotted, and more difficult with the barge."

One did not argue with Julius. I said, "Well, you will have a chance next year."

"If there is a next year."

There would only be a second expedition if this one failed. I thought of what failure could mean, to me personally. The diminutive valley of fields and houses and ribboned rivers, on which I had so often looked with longing, was as sunny as before, but suddenly less attractive. I was staring at it from a dark hole, but one in which I had come to feel safe.

Yet even in the brush of fear, I felt sorry for Henry. I could have been the one left behind. I did not think I would have borne it as well, if so.